"Like what you see, honey?"

Emma did, and it infuriated her. "I am not your honey."

"Your hair's like honey." Frazer's voice was thick and creamy, almost mesmerizing. "What were you doing climbing out of a strange window?"

"How do you know that's not my room?" Emma countered.

"I happen to know that yours is two rooms along. I know more about you than you realize, Emmaline Rainer."

"You didn't yesterday," she said.

"Before I met you I didn't care to know."

"And now you do. Why?"

Frazer's eyes glowed. "Honey, if you have to ask that, your female instincts are all shot to hell." And he tilted his body forward, his chest brushing her breasts, and kissed her, his mouth warm and soft....

Susan Napier was born on Valentine Day, so perhaps it is only fitting that she become a romance writer. She started out as a reporter for New Zealand's largest evening newspaper before resigning to marry the paper's chief reporter. After the birth of their two children, she did some free-lancing for a film production company and then settled down to write her first romance. "Now," she says, "I am in the enviable position of being able to build my career around my home and family."

Books by Susan Napier

HARLEQUIN PRESENTS

885—SWEET AS MY REVENGE
924—THE COUNTERFEIT SECRETARY
940—THE LONELY SEASON
1051—TRUE ENCHANTER
1093—REASONS OF THE HEART
1211—ANOTHER TIME
1252—THE LOVE CONSPIRACY
1284—A BEWITCHING COMPULSION
1332—FORTUNE'S MISTRESS
1380—NO REPRIEVE

HARLEQUIN ROMANCE

2711—LOVE IN THE VALLEY
2723—SWEET VIXEN

SUSAN NAPIER

deal of a lifetime

Harlequin Books

TORONTO • NEW YORK • LONDON
AMSTERDAM • PARIS • SYDNEY • HAMBURG
STOCKHOLM • ATHENS • TOKYO • MILAN
MADRID • WARSAW • BUDAPEST • AUCKLAND

Harlequin Presents first edition May 1992
ISBN 0-373-11460-5

Original hardcover edition published in 1991
by Mills & Boon Limited

DEAL OF A LIFETIME

CHAPTER ONE

'*CHILDREN?*'

'And babies. Buckets of them, by all accounts.'

Emmaline Rainer stared, horrified, at her super-efficient male secretary.

'But there can't be! This is supposed to be a working weekend, an opportunity to do some serious lobbying...'

Marc Fletcher corrected her scrupulously. 'All Sir Clive said was that he was going to put all the candidates through their paces, which is pretty ambiguous if you think about it. Evidently he meant socially as well as professionally. I suppose he wants to see how well you fit in with the wider family. After all, it is a family-owned business and his right arm has to be someone they generally approve of. They all have voting shares...'

'Well, why didn't he say so in the first place?' said Emma raggedly. 'I've worked day and night on these projections to have them ready in time!' She jerked on the handle of her elegant leather briefcase, her suddenly sweaty palm nearly losing its grip. 'I wanted a chance to lay them all out for him before that weasel Edward finds out what I've been doing and does some of his own. I'm finally one step ahead of the others and now I don't get a chance to prove myself? He can't do this to me!'

'As head of the company he can do what he damned well likes,' Marc pointed out drily. 'And frequently does. You still might get the opportunity to tell him your ideas——'

'With children clinging to my skirts? Oh, yes, that'll make a great impression,' Emma interrupted sarcastically. It was an image she had been trying to shake off through nearly all of her twenty-six years, that of an earth-mother, a female who properly belonged in the kitchen, bedroom or nursery, not the ruthless world of business. It wasn't that she wanted to be a man, far from it, but she resented the fact that the overt femininity of her full figure and ice-blonde hair was often used to denigrate her intelligence. 'Child-bearing hips'—how often had she had had that thrown at her, both as insult and imagined flattery, by smart-aleck male business colleagues? It wasn't her fault that she was short, nor that her sleek, clever business suits failed to smooth away the generous curves at breast and hip. Nor was it her fault that children seemed drawn to her like bees to honey. That didn't mean she wanted to spend her life smothered by them! Sir Clive Conway was fairly progressive in his outlook—witness his willingness to consider a woman not yet thirty for the position of his new executive director—but that was only because she carefully projected the right image: that of complete, asexual dedication.

'Maybe I could pretend to be sick!' She grasped at the straw. She certainly felt it—a stomach-churning sensation that this weekend was going to turn out to be a disaster for her career.

Marc glanced around the tiny terminal which served the seaplanes and helicopters that plied their mainly sightseeing trade around Auckland's harbour and environs. 'You've left it a bit late,' he said, 'unless you can come up with something really plausible like a heart attack. But who wants to promote someone with a dodgy heart?'

Emma glared at him in frustration. 'Why didn't *you* tell me earlier? I could have worked up a good case of something suitably innocuous.'

'I didn't know earlier. I just wheedled it out of Acid Addie. It's supposed to be another of the old man's cunning little manoeuvres to find out how you all react to unexpected situations.'

Adeline Marsh was Sir Clive's secretary and had been his father's before that. No one ever dared breathe the word 'retirement' in her presence, even though the rumour went that she was even older than her boss. Adeline was an institution, her tongue as sharp as her faculties. She was also as close as the grave.

'How on earth did you get it out of her?' Emma asked in admiration. She had coped with male chauvinism throughout her career and handled it with practised cool. Adeline could make her shake in her shoes.

'Oh, I just used my boyish charm,' said Marc modestly, and in spite of her worries Emma's mouth twitched in a smile. Marc was a year older than herself and definitely not a boy. He was ruggedly built, not handsome but undeniably masculine. He favoured expensive suits, always dark, and white silk shirts and his shoes were handmade. He also wore dark horn-rimmed spectacles whose studious air so perfectly balanced all his rugged virility that Emma sometimes wondered whether it wasn't just another piece of costume. One day she must take a peek at the glass in them. 'Actually, I didn't have to do a thing,' Marc confessed. 'I overheard her checking on the cargo that's going over to the island with us. Extra food supplies for the masses, baby-food included.'

Emma's stomach tightened anew. 'I think I *am* going to be sick!' She squared her padded shoulders, reminding herself of all the years of determined study and effort. Damn it, biology wasn't going to defeat her now, not when she was so close to her goal!

'What's the matter, Em? You look rather green. Afraid of flying, are we?'

'Thank you for your generous concern, Edward, but it's not *flying* that turns my stomach.' Emma turned smoothly to deflect the pointed dart back at the tall, husky, hatchet-faced man who had paused beside them, his decorative brunette wife attached to his arm.

'No? A little pre-menstrual tension, perhaps?' Edward Cleaver gave her a smile that was more of a sneer. 'We all know how you women have these emotional ups and downs. Why don't you let Marc come on alone? A clever secretary must be *such* a help when you get out of your depth, especially one who is so much more qualified than yourself... Why, I bet without Marc you'd be absolutely *lost*...' He sauntered away, content with the un-subtle suggestion that Emma wasn't the author of her own career.

'One of these days,' breathed Emma heavily through her teeth, 'I'm going to fire that man.'

'If he doesn't fire you first,' murmured Marc, re-minding her that Edward was a front-runner for the promotion she was angling for.

'How a man that obnoxious has got this far without someone squelching him underfoot I'll never know.' Emma's honey-brown eyes murdered the retreating back.

'He's only obnoxious to you, to the rest of us he's just a regular slimeball. Don't let him get to you, Emma, that's what he wants. And, after all, he was only telling the truth—I *do* have a better degree than you, and I *am* the one who does all the work. You're just along for decoration.'

Emma laughed. 'You're lucky I trust you, kiddo. If I thought you were really after my job I'd cut you off at the knees.'

She meant every word but Marc only grinned in reply. He was ambitious, he made no secret of it, but only up to a point. He played as hard as he worked, and wasn't willing to sacrifice his myriad outside interests for the kind of complete dedication that executive status in a large company demanded. Neither did he want to be in-hibited by the strictures imposed by the time-honoured rules of the promotion game. When she had hired him three years ago, he had frankly informed Emma that he was a 'born assistant', looking to ride someone else's coat-tails to the top. In return for a salary that would take into account both his impressive PhD in business administration and his affluent lifestyle, he could offer complete loyalty, a genius for ferreting out information, and a nose for trouble. All three had been proved time and time again, and Emma had never regretted her initial decision to top up his salary from her own during the six months before she gained enough financial autonomy in the legal division of ConCorp to officially recognise his worth. During Marc's reign in her outer office she had shot from executive underdog to a real contender for power and she knew that without his organisational brilliance it might well have been a much longer, less interesting slog. It was for Marc's sake, as well as her own, that she wanted this promotion. She had promised him a big, fat bonus if she got it. Enough for him to buy that Porsche he had his eye on.

'Emma.' Charles Scott, the other front-runner, gave her a brisk, indifferent nod as he strode past. He was in his early forties, an arch-conservative, and saw Emma not as a personal threat, but as the thin end of the wedge, an unwelcome disruption to the comfortable 'men's club' atmosphere that still pervaded most of the nation's boardrooms. His wife, Mary, who offered Emma a faded smile as they swept past, was the kind of woman that Charles admired: 'The Little Woman'—Emma had actually heard him refer to Mary in those words—quiet, loyal and supportive to her man, shaped and guided totally by her husband's opinions. The poor woman didn't even know she was downtrodden, she was so well brainwashed.

Emma followed reluctantly in their wake, still hoping for a miracle. It was Friday the thirteenth, wasn't it? Maybe every helicopter, plane and ferry in the city would be inexplicably out of action, or a hurricane suddenly blossom on the horizon.

No such luck. The evening remained as clear as a bell. Their bags were loaded on to the chartered helicopter and they were strapped into their seats, the rotors beginning to turn before the last two passengers arrived, flinging their cases into the passenger compartment before they clambered in. Jasper Teal and a young girl who didn't look much more than a fresh-faced teenager. Jasper was the wild card in the bunch, a rank outsider, even to a liberal thinker like Emma. For a start he was even younger than she was, albeit only a year, and he appeared a little too frequently in the gossip columns for anyone in a basically conservative company like ConCorp to take him seriously. He had plenty of brilliant ideas but he had no formal qualifications and in Emma's opinion was too high-spirited and self-opinionated to work comfortably in tandem with Sir Clive—or Steven Conway, Sir Clive's son, who was being groomed for eventual succession to the ConCorp Crown. She suspected that Sir Clive had only added Jasper to the select group to stir up the pot. He liked to keep his executives on their toes.

Jasper mouthed something she couldn't hear over the rising whine of the whirling blades—she doubted that he was apologising for his tardiness; he enjoyed playing the rebel too much to be sorry about ruffling a few feathers. He caught her disapproving stare and grinned, giving her a thumbs-up signal before leaning over to whisper in his companion's ear. She giggled. She was petite and attractive; Emma only hoped the girl was less innocent than she looked. If she didn't read the gossip columns she might not realise what she was letting herself in for. Jasper never seemed to date the same woman more than once. Probably because, with his dark good looks, he got all he wanted first time around.

Tiki Island, owned by the Conway Family Trust, was one of the island jewels in Auckland's Hauraki Gulf. Only a few square kilometres in size, it was a lush, peaceful retreat just twenty minutes' flying time from the city—an hour and a half by boat. Because it was privately owned there was little development there—a small stretch of farmland that was leased by one of the family, a few discreet pole-houses, which served as holiday homes for this cousin or that, vaulting out of the bush-clad north-side of the island, and a sprawling, low-lying collection of loosely connected forms that made up the main residence, which was large enough to house two dozen guests as well as the intermittently resident members of the Conway clan. Emma saw it all as the helicopter lazily circled the island. She had been to the island several times for business conferences but had met few of Sir Clive's family. The Conways were a close-knit lot, that was how they had managed to keep tight control of a very lucrative corporation, and Sir Clive didn't encourage fraternisation between his family and employees below a certain level.

The heli-pad was just outside the white concrete wall, topped with red tiles, that surrounded the main compound. A man, ducking to protect himself against the swirling down-draughts as the pilot switched off the rotors, unloaded their bags on to a small trolley. The eight passengers filed out of the big cabin, following the man with the trolley through a side door in the wall. The interior of the compound was not one large space bordered by buildings, as expected, but a series of cobbled walks walled on both sides by high lattice screens overgrown with jasmine, bougainvillaea, clematis and other leafy climbers ablaze with summer colour and scent. Large dragon pots filled with citrus and other dwarf fruit trees and shrubs studded the walks. The overall effect was of a meandering maze which encouraged exploration, but it wasn't until they arrived at an open plaza where a fountain played that Emma was tempted to take a wrong turning. Beyond the fountain was a door to the main house. Double doors, in fact, thrown open to reveal a cluster of people ready to welcome the arriving guests. One of them was Dorothy, Lady Conway, Sir Clive's wife, but most of the rest appeared to be children.

Emma detained Marc by his sleeve. 'You don't suppose there's another way in, do you?'

Marc lingered behind the screen of water as the others went on. 'I'm sure there is, but don't you think that might look rather odd?'

'We can say we got lost. Or that we couldn't resist a quick tour of the gardens. Come on, Marc, I'm not running the gauntlet yet,' she said, backing away. 'Sir Clive isn't a man to stand on ceremony himself, look— he's not even there himself to greet us. Chances are no one'll notice if we mingle in later. I think I saw a promising path back here...'

'You're only postponing the inevitable, Emma,' Marc pointed out with inescapable logic as they retraced their steps. 'You're going to have to meet the children some time.'

'Yes...well...' Emma hated her uncharacteristic panic. She had built her reputation on being firm and decisive at all times, made a career out of never leaving anything to chance, of always being prepared for the worst. And here she was practically dithering. No wonder Marc was surprised. 'If I can maybe contrive to be introduced to them singly rather than *en masse* I might be able to squeeze by without coming across like the Pied Piper. I'm relying on you to watch my back, Marc...down this way, here...'

'You want me to ride shotgun? Pick off the toddling bandits?' Marc grinned. He had seen the effect that his boss had on children and thus could sympathise with her dilemma, but he couldn't help also finding it amusing.

Emma scowled back at him as she pushed past a straggling grape vine. 'Whatever happens to me happens to you,' she reminded him. 'You've got a vested interest here to protect, Marc, unless you have plans to resign.'

'Whither thou goest, there go I,' he replied piously as they emerged abruptly beside a huge swimming-pool.

'Ah, I knew it!' announced Emma triumphantly, pointing to where a series of folding glass doors opened the whole rear of the house to the stone-paved pool area. 'There you are. An open invitation to a discreet entrance.'

As she stepped forward Marc threw his arm out in front of her. 'Hang on.' He made an elaborate production of looking around and then began to tip-toe ludicrously across the paving stones. 'All clear, boss!' He beckoned her with a furtive whisper.

'There are times, Marc, when your sense of humour is *not* appreciated,' Emma hissed quellingly, marching after him.

'Can I direct you somewhere? Or are you just casing the joint?'

Emma's low heel turned dangerously in a crack in the paving stones as she spun around. She staggered and recovered herself, flustered with embarrassment. Marc's steadying hand under her elbow annoyed rather than appeased her. It was his idiotic frivolity that had resulted in their being caught behaving like third-rate criminals. Now he was making her look like a clumsy female who wasn't even in control of her own body. She stepped away, wrenching her elbow free—another ill-judged movement, because now she teetered on the near edge of the pool. This time Marc didn't dare touch her and she was forced to windmill her arms to regain her balance, dropping her briefcase in the process. Fortunately it didn't fall in the water.

The man who had caused the mini-tumult stood unmoving throughout the whole charade. Emma found herself disliking him instinctively for being witness to her embarrassment, and for the casual way he dominated his surroundings. He was only moderately tall and very tanned, his dark blond hair worn in a shaggy cut which matched the trendiness of his attire. His vivid blue eyes were narrowed against the sharp reflection of the sun bouncing off the pool and a light brown stubble covered his slashing jaw. He wore a white linen jacket with the sleeves pushed up, and no shirt. The exposed part of his chest was almost hairless but there was no doubting his masculinity. The tanned skin was sculpted with muscle, his impressive shoulders obviously needing no padding under the softly constructed jacket. The experienced lines around his eyes and hard mouth put him somewhere in his late thirties. A tough customer. Emma sought a fresh handle for her dislike and found it with little trouble. Now she knew why her first glimpse of him had seemed familiar... in the white jacket, pastel blue trousers and designer stubble he looked for all the world like Don Johnson. He probably deliberately played on the likeness, especially with women. Well, *she* wasn't impressed. Didn't he know that the *Miami Vice* look was *passé*?

'We've just been strolling through the gardens——' she began cautiously, thinking it would be as well to find out who he was before she let her instinctive aggression show. He had all the hallmarks of a security man but the style of uniform was a bit over the top for Sir Clive.

'If you're Press doing some unauthorised snooping, I ought to warn you that Sir Clive has given me permission to throw you off the island,' he interrupted her with clipped rudeness as he speared a glance at the sophisticated camera that hung from Marc's shoulder. His eyes were hard as sapphires in their contempt. 'People like you let the whole profession down. If you'd rung for an appointment instead of barging in on his privacy Sir Clive would have been quite happy to give you an interview——'

So he *was* security. Well, that explained his rudeness...almost. And all that sickening macho cool. 'Of course we're not Press,' Emma cut in firmly. 'We're invited guests.'

Dark blond eyebrows rose sceptically. Emma could feel herself getting hot under the collar. She wasn't used to being disbelieved.

'We came in the helicopter with the others,' she gritted.

'Others?' He looked pointedly around the empty pool area.

'They went in the front entrance,' she explained slowly and methodically as if he were a moron. Perhaps his head was as packed with muscle as the rest of him.

He was undisturbed by her pointed condescension, revealing the determination of a bull terrier by worrying at the very point she had been trying to evade. 'While you came skulking around the back. Any particular reason for that?'

None that she was prepared to give this arrogant brute.

'Perhaps I'm shy,' Emma snapped sarcastically. It should have put him firmly in his place but instead his face went blank with puzzlement. Obviously sarcasm was beyond his ken. She would have to try another tack. 'I'm Emma Rainer, in charge of ConCorp's legal department...'

She trailed off expectantly but there was not a flicker of respect in the bland expression, nor any of recognition. Either he was an excellent poker player or he really was just plain dumb. And now she had violated one of the classic rules of one-upmanship, allowing his bullishness to manoeuvre her into revealing her identity before demanding his. She had no choice but to continue.

'This is my secretary, Marc Fletcher.'

This did get a reaction. The man gave Marc a fairly comprehensive once-over, noting the fine physique under the expensive lightweight suit, before swinging his gaze back to Emma's tight expression and murmuring in a tone redolent of mocking innuendo, 'Of course he is.'

Emma felt herself bristle. It wasn't the first time someone had implied that she and Marc were more than boss and secretary, nor would it be the last, but somehow, from this man, it was even more offensive than usual. She decided that the only way to redeem the situation was to turn the tables.

'May I ask by what right you interrogate Sir Clive's guests?'

'The right of curiosity,' he said. 'You must admit you were acting rather suspiciously.'

Emma's legal training advised her to admit to nothing of the sort, and she merely fixed him with the gimlet stare that served her so well in the office. The silence stretched uncomfortably until Marc decided to break the deadlock.

'That was just me fooling around.' He shrugged, taking the blame on to his own broad shoulders. Emma might have appreciated the effort if she hadn't noticed the sudden amused twitch of the blond man's mouth.

'Oh, you fool around together much, do you? I'd no idea that legal departments were such fun places to work.' The voice which had formerly been so cool and incisive suddenly dropped to a slow and honey-thick burr.

Marc made a queer choking noise but Emma had had enough of pussy-footing around. 'Look, are you on the security staff or not?' she demanded. 'If not I don't see why we should stand around being insulted. For all we know *you* might be the trespasser here. We've identified ourselves. Now who are *you*?'

He chose to play coy. 'Well, I *could* be one of the family, protecting my own,' he offered in that wretchedly attractive accent. The glint of mocking challenge in the deep blue eyes goaded Emma's disbelief.

'You look more like the type of man one protects one's family *against*,' she said tartly. Especially the female members, she thought. He must have read the thought in her speaking brown eyes because his mockery increased. He didn't fit any of the mental identikit pictures that Emma had formed over the years of Sir Clive's various male relations. And wasn't that burr a faint American drawl? There were no Americans dangling from the family tree. No, the man was obviously an employee of some kind, but one with a fair degree of autonomy.

'Whoever you are, you're not doing a very good job. While you're harassing legitimate guests a whole legion of thieves could have come and gone——'

'If they have, I'm sure you'd relish watching me get my walking papers,' he said, confirming her belief in his employed status. 'Perhaps you might even volunteer to do the job yourself. Do you get a thrill out of the act of dismissal?' He made it sound indecently erotic. 'Would you enjoy firing me, honey? Draw it out long and slow? Make it good for both of us...?'

Emma was outraged. He was laughing at her. Not so dumb after all. Emma hated being played for a fool. Especially by a cheap imitation cop. Normally she had nothing but contempt for people who abused their power over others, but for once she was tempted. Reporting his insubordination to Sir Clive would wipe that leer off his face. But no, she wasn't going to let him drag her down to his level! She was going to retain what was left of her dignity.

Emma snatched the briefcase that Marc had picked up for her and contented herself with a last, withering look before she strode away. She thought she heard a chuckle behind her but she refused to look back. She never looked back on her mistakes, she just learned from them and went on, a better person. And at least she had escaped without revealing her fear of children. That *would* give him something to laugh about.

'Do you think that was wise, antagonising him like that?' Marc murmured as they stepped inside the house. 'After all, he never did tell us who he was.'

'He was pretty antagonising himself,' said Emma, cautiously following the sound of voices through the inner rooms. The interior walls of the house were in the same white, rough-cast concrete as the exterior and the floors baked terracotta tile. The Mediterranean flavour was carried through in the arched doorways and sparse but solidly luxurious dark wood furnishings. 'If he turns out to be a trusted friend or something we'll just pretend it was all an amusing misunderstanding. We've got enough to worry about, Marc, without brooding about imagined problems.'

'It's just that I had this strange feeling that he looked familiar.'

'Don Johnson,' said Emma, pausing to see if she could detect any childish trebles in the adult rumble coming from the next room.

'Who?'

'You know. From that flash and dash American TV cop show. That's who he looked like. Don Johnson. A very jaded Don Johnson.' The last added out of pure maliciousness.

'I didn't know you watched programmes like that, Emma, I would have thought your feminist instincts would be outraged by the juxtaposition of all that sex and violence...' said Marc innocently.

Emma gave him a repressive look. 'The rerun is on straight after the late news; I happen to see it occasionally. I don't watch television much, I don't have time.' Usually she took a stack of work home from the office each night and Marc, better than anyone, knew that the latter half of her statement was true. However he didn't know that trashy late-night television programmes were her secret vice. After a hard day's—and evening's—work she loved to curl up in her big bed and sip a glass of milk and munch on crackers and scoff out loud at the plots of grainy old movies and hurl insults at the scriptorial inadequacies and clichéd charm of the second—and sometimes third-and fourth-hand series that inhabited TV's graveyard shift. It was a blissfully relaxed way to vent her real-life frustrations viciously and without fear of retribution.

'Mmm, well, it definitely wasn't Don Johnson that struck me,' Marc returned to ponder the problem. 'It wasn't a likeness to anyone famous, it was more of an *impression*. You know I never forget a face so I certainly haven't met him before, but there's just something about him. I'll let you know if it comes to me...'

'You do that,' said Emma dismissively as she stepped into a seemingly crowded room.

'Ah, there she is! Emma, everybody was just wondering where you had got to. Leave your briefcase in the chopper? Deborah's just about to show everyone their rooms. Come on, come on. Introductions will have to wait until later...'

Sir Clive was in bluff good humour; he had provided her with a perfect explanation for her obviously commented-on absence and there wasn't a child in sight.

Things were looking up!

CHAPTER TWO

'Hi.'

Emma blanched at the sight of the chubby little boy on a tricycle who had braked to a halt in the hallway as she opened her door. She knew her good luck had to run out some time. Last night's dinner had been a breeze, all children shuffled off to bed by the time the adults were called to dine.

'Hello,' she said coldly.

'I'm J-James. I'm f-five.'

'Really?' She injected a lethal note of boredom into her voice, debating whether to duck back into her room. J-James took her silence in good spirits and rushed eagerly into the breach with his bright, stuttering chatter. She already knew who James was: one of the Conways' grandsons. Lady Conway had told her all about them last night. She had misunderstood the shock with which Emma had received the news that six, *six* little Conways were loose in the house. Or, not quite Conways, as Lady Conway explained, assuming that Emma's expression of horror was one of wide-eyed fascination.

'I have no family myself but Clive more than makes up for my lack,' she had told Emma over coffee in the drawing-room when the men had aggravatingly retired for the Conway tradition of port and cigars. 'There were four brothers and four sisters from his father's two marriages, you know, but only two of the males survive— Clive and his brother, Frazer.'

When Emma's brow had wrinkled Lady Conway had side-tracked for a moment to add, 'Don't be surprised if you can't place Frazer, he's never had anything to do

20

with ConCorp and he's lived overseas for many years. Frazer was an engineer until a few months ago...but you're not interested in the senior Conway generation, you were asking about the younger tribe...' Leaving Emma with the impression that Sir Clive's brother must have recently retired from his profession. Emma knew that the other two Conway brothers had been killed in the Second World War and that one of the sisters had died during an influenza epidemic in the early forties. Sir Clive himself was sixty-eight, but still surprisingly robust considering his love of rich food and good whisky and the quantity of foul-smelling cigars that he puffed his way through every day. Perhaps Frazer Conway shared his brother's good health, but whether he was older or younger he would still be getting fairly well on in years.

'...The Conways have this unfortunate propensity—unfortunate, that is, as far as the arrogant males of the family are concerned——' Lady Conway had smiled, revealing a sense of humour as warm as the rest of her, '—of expanding along the female line. Do you know Clive and I have four granddaughters, two grandsons, seven nieces and one nephew, seven great-nieces and one great-nephew? And only *one* of the whole lot of them carries the surname Conway! That's why Clive is always hinting that Steven and Sheena should hurry up and have children. Miriam and Julie have given him a grandson each but that's not good enough. Oh, no, Clive wants a *Conway* boy. I suspect, Emma, dear, that if I weren't well into my dotage Clive would be urging *me* to have more sons!'

Emma began to walk briskly along the hallway. She had deliberately lingered in bed this morning, having been warned that the children were usually fed and watered long before the mid-morning brunch around the pool that was a feature of such weekends. It appeared she hadn't lingered quite long enough. As she strode she heard the ominous sound of a trike doing a fast U-turn behind her, and then it was squeaking along at her side.

'Are you coming out to p-play?'

'No.' Emma kept her gaze straight ahead, not wanting to meet the big brown reproachful eyes she could feel fixed on her unresponsive profile.

'I want to p-play.' An expectant pause. 'You look like the sun.'

'Really?' She supposed it was a compliment on her casual but elegant yellow cotton sun-dress but she refused to be bribed. 'Hadn't you better go and find your friends?' she told him.

'Have you got any little b-boys?'

'No.' It wasn't enough that children enjoyed talking to her. For some reason they were also fascinated by the details of her private life.

'G-girls, then?'

'No. I have no children at all,' she said, firmly dismissive. She had reached the end of the hallway and placed her hand against the glass-panelled door that opened on to the walkway which joined the guest wing to the main house.

'I could be your little b-boy while you're here. Then y-you won't be lonely.'

'I'm not lonely.'

'My mummy is lonely when she doesn't have anyone to p-play with. Do you have a d-daddy?'

'No!' She knew he meant husband. To a child his age all men of importance were daddies. She dropped her hand from the door. She knew that if she went through it, sure as eggs James was going to follow, spewing out his remorseless, intrusive and no doubt increasingly embarrassing questions. Everyone except Emma would be vastly entertained by his childish attachment. She made up her mind. She turned around and began to walk briskly back the way she had come. A few steps later she stopped dead. Ahead of her there were now three more trikes strung across the width of the hall. Three little girls of descending size regarded her with bright-eyed interest.

Emma looked behind her. James gave her a kind smile, forgiving her for her brusqueness. She took another step. As if it was a silent signal all four trikes began to slowly converge. It was absolutely ridiculous to be afraid of a few harmless infants but suddenly Emma felt claustrophobic. She took a few skipping side-steps and slipped inside the nearest room. She leaned against the closed door, her heart beating absurdly fast, listening. She could hear squeaking, then whispers, giggles, the not-so-gentle nudge of tyres against the wall outside the room.

'Emma, what on earth are you doing?'

Emma jumped as if she had been shot. It was Marc, coming out of his bathroom, bare-chested, holding a razor, shaving cream still on his chin. Thank goodness it was his room she had picked, she thought in relief. How on earth would she have explained herself to anyone else?

'There are children out there! They were waiting for me when I came out of my room. I tell you, Marc, they have some sort of built-in radar.'

'My God, Emma, they're only children!'

To Emma's horror Marc reached past her and threw open the door. 'Hi, kids!'

The four had dismounted their steeds. Their eyes, all remarkably similar shades of brown, moved from Marc to Emma.

'Is he your d-daddy?' asked James, with fascinated interest.

'I told you, I don't have a daddy. Now why don't you go away?'

'Why hasn't your daddy got his clothes on?' asked one of the dark-haired moppets who must have been all of four.

'Cos they're goin' to b-bed, Amy, *that's* why?' guessed James knowingly. For all his stammer he was obviously a fairly switched-on kid. 'Is that why you don't want to p-play? My d-daddy doesn't wear any clothes in b-bed and my mummy doesn't too.'

The smallest of the girls managed to get a handle on the situation. She pointed to Emma. 'Lady play!' she demanded.

'Marc, get rid of them,' said Emma, desperately edging behind him.

The littlest one stamped her foot. 'Play!' This time it was a command issued with all the imperiousness of her three years.

'Hey, now, poppet, Emma has things to do. You'd better run along.' Marc's voice had the slightly hearty air of pleading that seemed to afflict bachelors when they had to put their foot down with strange children.

'She's not poppet, she's Lizzie, she's my cousin,' said Amy, contemptuous of his ignorance. 'So is James, and Jessie.' She pointed to the silent member of the quartet who was content to stand and stare adoringly at Emma, thumb firmly in mouth.

'Whatever. Why don't you run along and find Mummy?'

'I want *her*!' Lizzie insisted, aiming a dramatic pudgy finger over his shoulder.

'Emma,' confirmed James with a nod. Emma gave an inward groan. Now they possessed the magic of her name there would be no stopping them, she knew from bitter experience.

'Just shut the door, Marc, don't get involved in a debate!' Emma said sharply. 'You'd only lose, anyway. Children can be incredibly stubborn. They'll be there all day if you give them any encouragement.'

'Don't be silly, they'll get bored and go away in a few minutes,' said Marc, tipping the children an apologetic wink as he closed the door in their bright faces. Emma made sure that she locked it, and was glad she had when the handle began to rattle.

Marc was forced to revise his opinion when the persistent knocking and calling and thumping continued unabated as he finished shaving. He still hadn't his shirt on when he came out of the bathroom to find Emma opening the window and standing up on the sill, hitching up the flowing skirt of her dress to thrust a leg over the lower, fixed part of the window.

'What on earth are you doing?'

'Going out the back way,' said Emma. 'You can brave the teeny troops if you like, but for goodness' sake don't tell them I've gone.'

'Emma——!' At that moment the telephone beside the bed began to burr and Marc went over to answer it.

The window was an aluminium one, opening outwards, and Emma had to go through it backwards and dangle, momentarily, above the flower garden as she tried to avoid catching her head. She gasped when her hips were suddenly clamped by a pair of warm hands. She automatically stiffened and began to kick and squirm but she was lifted effortlessly backwards away from the security of the rough-cast wall, the hands sliding from her hips to her waist to under her arms as she was lowered to the ground. She spun within the firm grasp and found herself staring up at a familiar tanned face.

'Been exploring again?' he enquired mockingly.

'None of your damned business,' she snapped, on firm ground again in more ways than one. When he hadn't turned up at dinner last night as an extra guest the vague anxieties that Marc had raised over their clash yesterday had subsided. She had been right and Marc had been wrong. 'Would you mind letting me go?' to her chagrin she heard shades of Lizzie in her command.

'Very much.' But his hands fell away and he stepped back. He was wearing indecently thin blue running shorts and a sweaty black T-shirt cut away at the shoulders.

Surprisingly, considering the harsh light of the morning, some of the lines that had etched his face in the mellow of last evening had faded. He looked revoltingly fit, obviously at the tail-end of a serious run around the compound. To Emma's horror she couldn't help appreciating the pure symmetry of his bared limbs. His arms and legs, tanned a shade darker than his face, were smothered with the dark blond hair that was so sparse on his chest. The muscles of his thighs were thick and hard. There was a light sheen of sweat over his entire body. The scent of him was heavy, boldly masculine. This morning he was clean-shaven, the blue eyes as vivid as she remembered.

'Like what you see, honey?'

She did, and it infuriated her. 'I am not your honey——'

'Your hair's like honey, a bleached clover honey that's like silk on the tongue——'

Emma was shocked by his imagery. She jerked her head away from the finger that tugged a strand from her neat chignon. 'My hair is not bleached——'

'And your eyes are like honey, too, the natural comb kind, a rich clear gold with hints of darkness...' His voice was thick and creamy, almost mesmerising. 'What were you doing climbing out of a strange window?'

'How do you know that's not my room?' she countered after briefly faltering at his abrupt transition from huskily outrageous flattery to crisp demand.

'I happen to know that yours is two rooms along. I know more about you than you realise, Emmaline Rainer.'

'You didn't yesterday,' she said. It was a good guess on his part but she was determined not to wince at the wretchedly old-fashioned Christian name that she had always tried to bury under the jaunty short form.

'Before I met you I didn't care to know.'

'And now you do. Why?'

His eyes glowed. 'Honey, if you have to ask that your female instincts are all shot to hell.' And he tilted his body forward, his chest brushing the tips of her breasts, and kissed her, his mouth warm and soft and satiny. Emma was so stunned she just stood there and let him do it. No man had stolen a kiss from her without at least her tacit permission since...since high school! It seemed intensely wicked and at the same time supremely innocent. He didn't try to part her lips, or use his tongue, or touch her in any other way. In fact, as kisses went, it was fairly chaste. So why did it set her head reeling?

He lifted his head and she saw, to her further confusion, that his eyes were far less innocent than his mouth. He knew exactly what he was doing to her. Her eyes fell away, denying him the acknowledgement he sought, and she received another shock. The running shorts which clung so brazenly to his sweaty loins now traced an unmistakably explicit outline beneath the flimsy blue silk. The kiss might have been physically chaste but his thoughts were most emphatically not!

Emma was momentarily speechless. Her first impulse was to say something weak and feminine like 'How dare you?' but he might feel obliged to tell her. Then she considered slapping his face, but that would credit the kiss with more importance than it deserved. She decided that the most crushing thing she could do would be to ignore it.

'Which way is the pool from here?' It was where the brunch was being laid out. She had known her way from the walkway but now she was feeling distinctly disorientated.

'Would you like me to escort you?'

'No, thank you,' she said hurriedly. 'Just point the way and you can...go about your business.'

'I thought I already was,' he murmured provokingly, watching her wide—too wide in her own opinion—mouth tighten ominously. 'Has anyone ever told you you're cute when you're mad?'

'Nobody who's lived to talk about it!' she snarled, and would have shoved past him if Marc's head hadn't suddenly appeared out the window.

'Sorry about that, Emma, did you need some help——? Oh! Hello...Mr...er...'

The man beside Emma didn't take up the hint. He was too busy looking at Marc's hurried attempts to put on the shirt that had been hanging off one arm and blot away the last of the shaving cream. Emma couldn't believe it when she saw her suave secretary actually blush under that savage scrutiny. Emma felt herself beginning to share his embarrassment. She, who never blushed, could feel one stealing betrayingly up her throat. The sapphire eyes snapped back to her, catching her in full flush and drilling holes in her already threadbare poise.

'Looks like someone's slipped up in the arrangements,' he said, with a cynical contempt that struck her oddly like a blow. 'Wouldn't adjoining rooms be more convenient? Lady Dorothy would be horrified at the thought of her guests having to use the windows to visit each other... I'm sure she wouldn't object if I transferred you to a suite...'

'*I* would object,' said Emma with icy distinctness, her blush draining rapidly away at the thought of this little incident filtering back to the others. Lady Dorothy was frank and generous, a likeable woman and tolerant hostess, but Emma knew that she had distinct views on the laxity of modern morals. Her daughters, Miriam and Julie, thirty-eight and thirty-seven respectively, had last night confided that even now their mother expected them to adhere to certain standards of behaviour laid down in their childhood. After complaining wryly about the way the restrictions had dogged them during their teenage years, the sisters now agreed that they were grateful for her insistence on self-discipline and self-respect. Sir Clive, too, had a streak of the Puritan in him, which was why he preferred his senior executives to be married. Another handicap for Emma, who hadn't had a 'steady' male friend since that hypocritical rat, Phillip, had almost caused her to make the worst mistake of her life.

'Why? Do you get your kicks out of sneaking around? Isn't there any satisfaction in an affair that's open and above board?'

Emma swore. 'We are not having an affair!'

'Mind your mouth, honey, I don't like women who swear——'

There was always one law for men...she bet that wicked mouth knew a few choice words! 'Good. That makes us even. Because I don't like sweaty hulks pawing me!'

Marc nearly fell out of the window. 'What? You mean he actually——? Hey, Emma, are you OK?'

'Calm down, pretty boy, I didn't lay a hand on her. Did I, Emma?' Hands on hips, he challenged her with his knowing smile.

Not a hand, no. She glared at him. She couldn't accuse him of that kiss without admitting her own complicity. Marc wouldn't understand why she hadn't shrivelled the wretch with a few well-chosen words. She wondered herself, and she didn't like the answers she was getting.

'Emma?' Marc, attuned to her moods, sensed the tension.

'It was a figure of speech,' she snapped lamely. 'Are you coming or not, Marc? I'm getting hungry.'

'Great. That was Trudy on the phone, reminding us. Uh...I think I'll use a more conventional exit.' He looked glad to escape the awkwardness outside the window. 'Hang on a minute.'

He disappeared and Emma heard a brief chorus of questioning trebles filtering through from the hall as he cautiously opened the door to his room and slipped out.

'Excuse me,' Emma addressed a broad, mucsled shoulder.

'Almost anything, Emma,' he said smoothly. He swept her a bow and stood aside. At the last minute he put out a splayed hand, almost touching her heaving breasts as he halted her. 'Almost,' he reiterated softly. 'I don't excuse lying and I don't excuse hypocrisy. Remember that next time we meet.'

'On the contrary, I'm going to do my very best to forget every single thing about you.'

His mouth curved in amusement. 'You might find that more difficult than you imagine. See you around, honey.' And he jogged off, flaunting his tight backside in the skimpy shorts, the rest of him moving in fluid co-ordination.

Emma closed her eyes. More than difficult—impossible. In the dark she could still see the shifting muscles in that magnificently lithe body, smell his arrogant male scent, and the intriguing flavour of him still lingered on her lips.

Her eyes snapped open. She was horrified. She never fantasised about the men she came into personal contact with...only with fictitious characters, or about men who were safely out of reach. That way she never had to fear the appalling consequences of her hormones suddenly raging out of control. And yet here she was practically drooling over a man who was all too obviously within reach, and whom she had instinctively disliked on sight. It was degrading. It was beneath her. Emma was no snob, but there was no getting away from the fact that she could never have a public liaison with someone like, like... What's-his-name. She would be laughed out of the boardroom—presuming she ever got there! Men could date their social and intellectual inferiors, even marry them, and it only reinforced their preening masculinity. If a woman did the same she was treated with sly contempt or pitying amusement. It was taken as evidence of poor judgement. No matter how clever or successful the woman, the man was still perceived as setting the standard for the quality of a relationship. Unfair, but a fact and one that Emma was acutely aware of. So what was happening to her? Was resolute celibacy finally taking its toll? Was she going crazy? The short answer must surely be yes.

Her appetite gone, Emma only nibbled at the sumptuous buffet laid out on long tables under the shady, vine-covered trellis that jutted out from the house. Smaller tables, covered with starched white tablecloths, were scattered under a cluster of striped umbrellas. Most of the others were already eating when Emma and Marc arrived so they had had to take pot luck in the pecking order. Edward, she noticed, had established himself and Christine at Sir Clive's table, and Charles and Mary were busy buttering up Steven. At thirty-five, he was physically a younger version of his father, but in Emma's opinion he didn't have the same instinctive flair for business. He was meticulous rather than opportunistic in his approach to new investments. The company would undoubtedly be safe under his stewardship, but it would lack the aggressive drive that his father had stamped it with.

His wife, Sheena, was a former model and Emma would be quite content if she didn't have to converse with her again this weekend. Sheena was a beautiful redhead but her beauty was only skin deep. At dinner last night she had revealed a wit that had often verged into bitterness, and the sulky droop to her perfect mouth hinted at an abiding discontent. Some people, it seemed, were never satisfied with what they had. Steven was a nice, and thoroughly honest man, and he treated his wife's scathing cynicism with more tolerance than Emma thought she deserved.

Jasper was happily flirting with Miriam and Julie while their husbands, Michael and Chester, both successful businessmen in their own right, looked on in amusement. It didn't bother Jasper that the two women were probably fifteen years his senior and it obviously didn't bother anyone else, either. They probably all realised that Jasper's flirtations were scrupulously fair—even Lady Conway had enjoyed her share of skilful flattery. Sometimes it took Emma an effort to remind herself that under that playboy lightness was a shrewd, heavyweight brain. One day, if he wasn't side-tracked by his own weaknesses, Jasper would be a formidable business ally... or opponent.

Trudy was the only one floating free, and the way she latched on to Marc when he and Emma appeared was an indication that the phone call had been prompted by a bit more than just politeness. Emma picked at her food and listened with amusement to the first delicate probings of two people trying not to seem too interested in each other. Trudy seemed rather young for a twenty-year-old, but if she had worked for Jasper for a few weeks and hadn't fallen in love with him, as most of his secretaries did, then she wasn't quite the vulnerable little thing she appeared to be.

So entertained was Emma by the budding romance that she didn't notice the approaching children until it was too late. Though they were hardly children, she was reassured to realise, as the two girls and a boy introduced themselves as Sir Clive's sister Joan's grandchildren. They were all in their early teens and Emma knew she could afford to relax a little, since even the most delicate hint to adolescents that they might not be wanted was usually enough to offend their dignity and send them on their way.

Still, not wanting to get too involved, she let their youthful good spirits dominate the conversation while she rediscovered her appetite and acted as a soundingboard for their unformed opinions.

Suddenly the boy jumped to his feet with a whoop of glee.

'It's Great Uncle Frazer!'

Emma, her back to the newcomer, watched the boy bound off and the two girls begin to preen. Frazer Conway must be a merry old soul, she concluded, to prompt such a positive reaction. The teens treated Sir Clive with a casual respect and affection which never overstepped the mark into uncool enthusiasm. But then, of course, they saw a lot of their New Zealand relations.

'I thought he lived in America,' said Emma, brushing the crumbs of a blueberry muffin from her lips.

'Oh, yes, he does, but he flew over yesterday,' said one of the girls breathlessly, rising with more aplomb than her cousin. 'Great-Aunt Dorothy wouldn't let us see him because she said he was pooped after the flight and wanted to sleep around the clock. He doesn't look pooped to me. Isn't it rad, having a great-uncle like Frazer?' She gave a swooning sigh that made Emma swivel around in her chair to get a look at this avuncular marvel.

Her mouth fell open and stayed that way for several drying seconds. It couldn't be! She felt herself melting into the chair. 'That's Frazer Conway?' she croaked. 'Him?' She didn't dare point. 'Sir Clive's brother?' No, surely not. For one thing, he was a generation short of years. For another, Emma couldn't face the prospect of having made an abject fool of herself.

'Yep, that's the old man!' The girl laughed at her shock. It was obviously a common reaction. 'I told you he was rad!'

He had changed his jogging gear for white trousers and a loose-fitting white shirt with a gathered yoke that might have looked feminine on any other man but on his hard frame merely accentuated the virility it cloaked. He was shaking Christine Cleaver's hand and smiling politely into her flustered face while Lady Conway flut-

tered proprietorially in the background. Emma choked
on her rising anger. He had never smiled with such cor-
rectness at *her*. No, Emma he had done his best to insult
and annoy and . . . and . . . *toy* with! Well, if he expected
her to grovel an apology he would have a long wait! And
he had the bare-faced gall to tell her that he didn't approve of lying and hypocrisy!

It was too much to hope for that Lady Conway would
not spy Emma, her chair shifted cunningly back into the
shade of her umbrella, especially since the two girls
beside her were practically hopping up and down in their
impatience for the formalities to be over with, waving
at their great-uncle as he made his way from group to
group for all the world as if he were a celebrity doing
the rounds of his adoring fans. Even the men seemed to
respond eagerly to his pleasant overtures.

'And last but not least, this is Emma Rainer,' Lady
Conway announced when Frazer had embraced his two
great-nieces and reduced them to giggles with his com-
pliments and promises of gifts from his suitcase. 'Emma,
this is my brother-in-law, Frazer.'

Lady Conway looked expectantly at Emma, almost as
if she were waiting for a round of applause. Emma was
very tempted to yawn. Instead she rose, avoiding the vivid
blue eyes, and held out her hand unenthusiastically.

Lady Conway rushed bracingly into the little silence
that ensued. 'You're probably wondering about the age
gap—everyone else has asked. Poor Frazer, it's been such
a trial to him, being younger than his own nieces. But
his mother married Clive's father the same year that Clive
and I got married—she was much younger than Thomas,
of course—and Frazer was born in the same year as Julie,
but several months later. Miriam and Julie used to boss
him around dreadfully when they were all growing up,
didn't they, Frazer?'

'And still do,' said Frazer, with such a lazy warmth
in his voice that Emma thought she might have mis-

judged him. Perhaps jet lag had affected him yesterday, and earlier. He hadn't taken her outstretched hand yet and she was forced to look at him to find out why. The laziness was all in his voice. His eyes were alert and challenging, assessing...

'Hello again, Emma,' he said deliberately and, having achieved his aim, finally took her hand in his. He held it firmly enough so that she couldn't draw it away without a struggle. They measured looks over the tingling contact.

Lady Conway looked almost crestfallen. 'You mean you've met before? But when? Why didn't you say something, Frazer? I didn't know you'd been to the States, Emma?'

'Oh, our acquaintanceship is very much in the infant stage,' drawled Frazer, and Emma held her politely blank expression with difficulty. Was he the kind of man who enjoyed kissing and telling? He could destroy her credibility at a stroke and they both knew it. She tensed, and he felt the contraction ripple down her arm to the fingertips curling in his grasp. He briefly enjoyed his moment of power, knowing he was going to relinquish it for the sake of the greater power to come. 'We met yesterday. I took a stroll just after I arrived, before I hit the sack. I ran into Emma right here, as it happened...'

'He accused me of trespassing,' Emma said coolly, recovering herself, quick to perceive that if she played his game she was allowing him to make the rules. 'We were quite rude to each other.'

'You were rude. I was merely...intrigued,' he murmured provocatively. Emma's thick lashes flickered as she made a career decision. To hell with what Lady Conway thought! She tightened her fingers around his hand and when he responded with a similar show of strength she dug her beautifully shaped nails deep between his knuckles. He winced, startled by the unexpected femininity of the attack, and she whipped her hand away, tucking it behind her back.

'No more than I, since you didn't see fit to introduce yourself,' she said pointedly.

'I didn't want to embarrass you,' he said kindly and watched her simmer.

'Oh, dear.' Lady Conway looked from one to the other, more flustered than Emma had ever seen her. But only for a moment. Then she reverted to her comfortable self, her dark brown eyes twinkling in her gently rounded face. 'Well, you have the rest of the weekend to resolve any early awkwardness. Just remember, Emma, that Frazer wasn't quite himself yesterday. He had a ghastly flight over, didn't you, dear? He was downgraded from business to economy because of some overbooking and was put beside a mother with two upset toddlers and a baby. Poor Frazer didn't get a wink of rest...'

Poor Frazer? When Emma flew anywhere she naturally went economy, but of course a Conway wouldn't have to worry about financial considerations. It must have been a nasty shock for him to have to share the rigours of the ordinary traveller's lot. Emma's lack of sympathy showed in her congealed gold gaze and disinterested murmur of condolence.

'Don't you have days, Emma, when just nothing seems to go right for you?' he enquired innocently, his blue eyes glinting with laughter as she stiffened. 'Days when all your luck seems to just...climb out the window?'

She was rescued from the fearful knowledge that she might have pushed her luck too far by Sir Clive, who rolled up to clap his brother on the shoulder. He had to reach up to do it.

'So, you've met the baby of the family, Emma. What do you think of him?'

Blond eyebrows rose, one corner of a sensuous mouth chiselled a blunt curve of amusement. 'A leading question if ever I heard one, Clive. What do you expect the poor girl to say? That I'm a dream come true?'

A nightmare more like, her eyes flashed obliquely at him. 'I'm sure your brother is a very fine man,' she lied smoothly through her teeth. 'Although he's stretching a point to call me a "girl". It's been years since I was stuck with that particular demeaning label.' Except by Edward. The two men would probably make great pals.

'It was meant as flattery, not insult,' Frazer responded just as smoothly.

'I don't consider it very flattering to be called immature,' said Emma tartly. 'Any more than you would be pleased to be called a "boy" at your age.'

'I should hope I retain some elements of boyishness in my character to balance myself as a man. The innocence of childhood is a very precious part of anyone's life, a necessary one, too, if we want to develop into happy adults. In fact, that quality of innocence and trust could do a lot to temper the cynicism and intolerance of so-called mature behaviour.'

Somehow, in a few short words, he had managed to make Emma sound petty and jaded and humourless. She wouldn't underestimate him again. This man could put 'Meat' Cleaver in the shade when it came to undermining an opponent's integrity.

'Are you here on a visit?' she asked, boldly changing the subject without giving any sign of her chagrin.

He inclined his head in admiration at her cool ability to cut her losses and it was left to Sir Clive to reply.

'Oh, no. Frazer is back in New Zealand for good. He's staying with us until he finds his own place. You'll probably be seeing a lot of him around, Emma.' He chuckled at some private joke. Emma hoped it wasn't at her expense. Sir Clive was no fool. He must have noticed that she and his brother rubbed each other up the wrong way.

It was all Emma could do to maintain her conversation over the next few minutes with polite monosyllables as Lady Conway gushed and Sir Clive beamed and Frazer Conway managed to look insufferably modest as his brilliant career first as a field engineer and latterly as a consultant was dazzlingly portrayed by his proud relatives. Brilliant he might be in his chosen profession, and handsome as the devil but that didn't make him *likeable*, thought Emma darkly, giving an inward sigh of relief as Sir Clive finally began to steer his brother away.

Frazer resisted long enough to say, in a mocking aside. 'Don't sulk, honey, it doesn't suit you. That mouth wasn't built for pouting.' His tone told her what he thought it *was* built for and she was annoyed to felt herself tingle in remembrance of his kiss.

'What? What was that?' Sir Clive was getting on, but there was nothing wrong with his hearing.

Frazer raised his voice. 'I was just telling Emma how fresh and beautiful she looked.'

'What?' Sir Clive frowned thoughtfully at Emma and she wished that she hadn't given in to a summery impulse when she had reached into her wardrobe that morning. She should have found some of her nice, neutral pastels instead of this bright statement of individuality. His frown cleared. 'Oh, yes, yes. Emma always looks as smart as a whip.'

Emma smiled, sinking back into complacency. It was more of a compliment on her intelligence and attitude than on her looks, which was exactly the way she wanted it.

'None of your shenanigans with Emma, now, Frazer,' she was delighted to hear him continue. 'I have plans for Emma...'

'So have I,' murmured Frazer, as he allowed himself to be towed away, and the cryptic comment took some of the shine off the little nugget of gold she had just received.

Her leap of hope did not go unnoticed. Edward cornered her as the staff were clearing away the remains of brunch.

'What's going on, Emma? What's this Frazer guy here for——?'

'He's family. And I guess he still considers this his home——'

'Don't go coy on me, Emma,' Edward cut in impatiently. 'You know what I mean. What's his place in the scheme of things? Why in the hell is the old man suddenly acting so smug? And have you noticed that he hasn't addressed two words to Steven all morning?'

Emma hadn't. She had had too many problems of her own to worry about Steven's, but she wasn't going to let Edward know her vigilance had lapsed. 'Are you suggesting that we pool our resources, Edward?'

'So you do know something!' he reacted predictably, his greatest weakness.

'I'm as much in the dark as you are,' said Emma, knowing he wouldn't believe her. Edward was too much a game player not to suspect that everyone else was trying to double deal.

However, he was right. Something was definitely brewing, she thought a little later as she wandered back to her room. So preoccupied was she that she forgot about her unconventional exit an hour or so previously and ran slap bang into the brat patrol. One of them, Jessie of the silent adoration, was crying. James had 'accidentally on purpose' run over the ladybird she was watching, with his tricycle, 'to see what would happen'. The predictable happened and James had remorsefully scraped up the remains and offered a proper burial but Jessie was proof against such blandishments. She had cried louder, and when James had hit her to make her shut up she had started to run to tell her mother but had tripped over, scraping her bare toe and breaking one of the flower-filled pots. Seizing his chance, James had offered to take her to 'that Emma' instead of seeking Julie, since Jessie's mother might be 'real mad' at her for breaking one of Grandpa's pots.

Emma could be hard-hearted when necessary but even she wasn't such a selfish witch as to send the sobbing Jessie on her way without even a kind word. She dabbed at the tiny scratch with cotton wool in her bathroom and kissed the wound, reminding herself of the recent article which had stated that 'kissing better' was rooted in scientific fact. A loving kiss, she had read, stimulated the brain into releasing a kind of natural chemical pain-killer to the site of the injury. It was scientific reasoning, not maternal instinct, that prompted her to kiss and cuddle the woebegone little girl until a watery smile broke out!

Then, of course, she had to inspect the steam-rollered ladybird and pronounce it indeed dead, mop up sympathetic tears from Lizzie and Amy, find the little ornate cardboard pillbox she stored her ear-studs in to serve as a casket and say a few appropriate words, including an oath of secrecy, as the tiny creature was buried in one of the dragon pots in a secluded part of the grounds…all on the understanding that Emma would be left alone for the rest of the day.

Amy, Sir Clive with dimples and pigtails, conducted the negotiations with remarkable skill. It was agreed that only in a strict emergency was Emma to be disturbed from her 'very important business'. In return she would take the blame for breaking the pots, because 'grown-ups get away with lots of b-bad things because they're grown-ups' as James explained earnestly.

Emma thought it was a pretty fair bargain. She only wished a certain other person would be as co-operative in staying away!

CHAPTER THREE

EMMA glanced guiltily around the empty dining-room and leaned forward to pick up the name card that sat on the plate to the right of hers.

Frazer Conway.

Quickly she switched the little ornately printed card with Marc's, which was two settings down, skipping Christine Cleaver's.

Then she frowned. Even that was too close. She took the card right down and around the other end of the table. Ah, Jasper...he would be a nice, safe bet. And swapping with him would put Frazer next to Sheena, which was all he deserved, and more... But that would put Trudy on the other side of him, and Emma had noticed that Marc wasn't too keen on Trudy's interest in the handsome new Conway arrival. She changed Christine for Trudy, only that meant Christine was next to her husband so she had to move Edward, and then one or two others to even things up.

By the time she had finished her frantic repositionings, only Sir Clive at one end of the table, and Lady Conway at the other, remained inviolate and Emma's heart was beating fast, her palms clammy as she hurried to join the others in the drawing-room for pre-dinner drinks. She had worked hard to develop a cool head in a crisis and was dismayed at the way it suddenly kept letting her down.

She knocked back her first calming drink a little too rapidly and then noticed Edward watching her avidly. All she needed now was for him to suggest she was a closet alcoholic!

41

'Is something wrong, Emma? You look a little...disturbed.'

She was being assailed from all sides. 'I'm just wondering what Edward's been plotting,' she told Charles quite truthfully. 'Marc told me that he and Sir Clive met in the library an hour ago for a private chat...'

Charles's solid, square face took on an expression of overbearing smugness. 'You mean Clive hasn't spoken to you yet? Oh, dear... He and I had quite a session this afternoon and I understand he's seeing Jasper in the morning. And you haven't even received notice yet? Ah, well...I suppose Clive has some sort of system. If it isn't ladies before gentlemen, perhaps it's in order of importance...'

If Edward hadn't had his eagle eye still on her Emma would have had another stiff drink. Since when had Charles dropped that honorific 'Sir'? She wondered whether Edward was also on first-name terms with the old man. That would just make her day!

Julie Masters provided a much-needed feminine diversion from her brooding thoughts, and got rid of Charles, by coming over to ask Emma where she had bought her dress.

'My mother made it,' Emma confessed with some pride, looking down at the sleek black silk taffeta dress which played up her sophistication while playing down the earthy attractions of her figure. Not an easy feat.

'She must be a marvellous seamstress!' Julie envied. 'Miriam and I are hopeless at sewing.'

They could afford to be! So, now, could Emma, but she knew her mother liked to feel needed. 'She is. She made this from scratch. I chose a picture from a fashion magazine and my mother drafted off the pattern and made it up for me.' Not without protesting, for Hazel Rainer hadn't thought that the style was 'right' for her eldest daughter. Emma's mother still hadn't adjusted to the fact that her nice little Emmaline was a high-powered executive in a big corporation. She longed for her daughter to 'settle down' to a 'normal life', which of course meant marriage and lots of babies.

An innocuous discussion of clothes followed, during which Emma noticed Frazer's late arrival and made sure that she kept well away. As they were called into dinner the older woman took her off guard by saying suddenly, 'By the way, if the children pester you again, don't hesitate to tell them to buzz off.' She smiled wryly at Emma's momentary loss of poise. 'I gather there's some secret involved that I'm not to be told, but Lizzie and James were singing your praises to the heavens when I tucked them in and I had to bribe Jessica into snuggling down with *four* stories instead of the usual two. She wanted you to come and say goodnight but I knew you were probably busy getting ready for dinner. What on earth did you do to become so popular so fast?'

'I wish I knew,' murmured Emma. If she did she might be able to avoid doing it again!

As everyone sorted themselves out around the big polished dining-room table Emma allowed herself a moment of quiet triumph. For the sake of appearances she allowed Trudy to draw her attention to her place and sat down, murmuring to Steve on her left. The chair on her right was scraped back and she turned to smile at Marc.

'Emma.' Frazer Conway acknowledged her with a brief nod as he sat down.

'You can't sit there!' she told him with haughty satisfaction. 'There's a seating plan.' She pointed officiously at the little folded rectangle in front of him. He picked it up and studied the curving print. Then shrugged and turned it around to display the printed name.

Frazer Conway.

Emma was enraged to have all her sweated labour undone. 'You switched cards!' she accused him in a voice as furious as it was low.

'How do you know?'

'Because I...' She stuttered to a halt. 'Because I looked in earlier,' she said weakly. 'Marc is supposed to be sitting next to me.'

'Emma, Emma...' he admonished her softly. 'You didn't just look in, you sneaked in and swopped me for your lover, didn't you?'

'He is not my lover,' she hissed through the corner of her set smile. 'And what makes you think *you* were supposed to be sitting there?'

'Because I sneaked in here before you and made *sure* I was. But I don't feel obliged to lie about it. I told you how I feel about lying, Emma.'

'You——!' Her eyes narrowed to golden sparks of fury at being thwarted. 'Don't you lecture me about honesty— you pretended to be a security guard——'

'I didn't pretend, you assumed. I got the impression you were really just using me as a punching bag for your frustrations. In fact, I've been watching you today, Emma, and it strikes me that you're constantly looking over your shoulder. You're far more edgy than any other of Clive's pet executives, and for no good reason that I can tell. You seem to have a hell of a lot going for you, in spite of the handicap of being a woman.'

He didn't give her a chance to bristle. 'It's as if you're trying to hide something, and if it's not an illicit relationship with Fletcher, what is it? You haven't by any chance been involved in a little embezzling, have you?'

'No, I have not!' she said, her commendable calm due solely to the fact he was so very wrong. 'And since you have nothing whatsoever to do with ConCorp I'd be obliged if you'd keep your dangerous speculation to yourself.'

'But I do... I am a shareholder, after all. I have quite a hefty interest in ConCorp... and it's growing by the minute.' She glared at him. 'Now, smile at Dot, before she puts two and two together and figures out that we conspired to wreck her table setting.'

Emma's gaze flickered to the end of the table and she felt a wave of renewed guilt as she saw her hostess looking around at her seated guests with a faint frown of bewilderment. Emma wasn't quite quick enough to look away when the brown eyes reached her, and she hastily summoned up a false smile. Beside her she heard Frazer give a warm chuckle and his sister-in-law stared at him thoughtfully, her frown clearing. She looked back at Emma and smiled with a hint of conspiracy.

'Now look what you've done,' said Emma crossly. 'You've made her think there's something going on.'

'There is.'

'Not on my part, there isn't.' Emma pointedly turned towards Steven and engaged him in a conversation about the island that lasted through the first course—lamb cutlets in tamarillo sauce. When the soup arrived Emma touched on a matter of mutual interest at ConCorp and to her dismay Steven looked uneasy, and stiffly steered them back into social inanities, drawing Mary Scott from his other side into the conversation.

Frazer had been merely biding his time. 'Sulking again, Emma?' he murmured as she stared thoughtfully into her soup.

'I never sulk.' Her chin lifted haughtily. It was against her very nature to ignore a challenge like that. 'It's so unproductive.'

'And is everything you do designed to be productive?' Frazer asked curiously.

'Yes.' Everyone had been warned to dress for dinner and Frazer's dark suit was no different from any of the other men's. His unobtrusive conservatism was disconcerting. Was this the same man who lounged around in clothes that looked as if they had come from the wardrobe department of a film studio? In her mind Frazer Conway was already indelibly labelled as an inveterate troublemaker, a man who refused to conform in either manners or dress to what was expected of him. She didn't like to think that she might have been wrong about him.

'That's rather sad. What do you do for fun?'

'Fun?' Emma repeated, as if she'd never heard of the word.

'Yeah, you know, to wind down after a tough day at the salt mines?'

She thought of trashy TV programmes and cracker crumbs in the sheets. Oh, yes, he would find that very amusing. She thought of baking, another secret vice. Let a man discover that you could cook like a dream and he'd have you chained to the kitchen in no time flat, never mind if you had a brain like Albert Einstein. 'I listen to music, I read...' She tried to think of something else equally non-sexist, and failed.

'All that excitement, how do you stand it?' he murmured.

'I get enough excitement in my work,' she said primly.

He grinned. 'Where do you find the most excitement, *on* your desk or behind it?' And while she was choking into her wine, he added smoothly, 'Of course, I mean in the work itself or in the power it brings you?'

To her embarrassment her spluttering drew all eyes and Edward took the opportunity to say, with a cunning combination of condescension and piety, 'Drinking too fast again, Emma? You know, you ought to take care, a small woman doesn't have the same tolerance of alcohol as a man. A few hurried drinks before dinner, a few glasses of wine...it all adds up without your realising it.'

Emma sensed rather than saw Frazer open his mouth and rushed into the breach. She didn't need defending, or pre-empting.

'Oh, I always keep a count,' she stated smoothly, 'but for the sake of the calorific, not the alcohol content. I like to keep to a healthy, balanced diet. You obviously don't realise it, Edward, but alcohol is very fattening,' with a tiny, flicking glance at the slight executive paunch that he was constantly struggling to control. Sir Clive's small grunting laugh provided her with the impetus to continue sweetly, 'A greater tolerance can actually be more dangerous than none at all because it can blind you to the damage you're doing to your body. You may think you're just putting on a little weight, but you're also killing off your brain cells. That's why I believe in moderation, whether you're small like me or...er...a lot larger...' Fat and brain-dead...for a subtle insult, Emma didn't think that was bad!'

'Very neatly done,' said Frazer admiringly under cover of the humorous argument she had triggered. 'Were you born with a sting in your tail, or did you develop that poisonous tongue in law school?'

'I didn't need it at university. Men and women compete on equal intellectual terms there. It seems to be out in the real world, with real money and real prestige up for grabs, that men rediscover their misogynistic roots. Just because I'm a woman I should be soft and easily domi-nated...' Her expression showed her contempt for the attitude.

'There are some men who find the reverse attractive,' said Frazer, and Emma looked at his straight face sus-piciously. She didn't believe for a minute that he was one of them, not when she added up the total sum of his infuriatingly sexist comments.

'I don't happen to think that either sex should domi-nate a relationship. I don't see why they can't operate in a field of mutual respect. I'm talking about a *business* relationship,' she added sternly, making it clear this was not an intimate conversation.

'Oh, of course. I totally agree,' he murmured meekly, his eyes shimmering with lazy laughter at her disbelief. 'Tell me, are you an only child, or perhaps the eldest?'

'No, to both,' she said, pleased to crush yet another of his assumptions. He was implying that her strength was the result of an accident of birth rather than of conscious will. 'I have two elder brothers, both farmers, and two younger sisters.'

'I would never have thought you came from a large family,' he said musingly. 'You don't have the...'

'Warmth?' People often accused her of being cold, just because she was cautious. But she had learned the hard way that it was better to be too cautious than too trusting, that if you didn't make it clear from the start how you expected things to be then people were prone to invest you with their own unreasonable expectations.

'Oh, I don't doubt your warmth, Emma. In fact I've seen you positively hot under the collar several times,' he said with a quick grin. 'I was going to say the *gregariousness* that growing up in a big family normally engenders. You seem to always be on the defensive with people. And I've noticed that when children are mentioned you get a peculiar, glazed expression on your face, as if you're bracing yourself for something nasty. I saw you with Nick and Mattie and Clare at brunch, three really nice kids, but you sat back and let them do all the work, as if you didn't quite know how to respond. Don't you like children, Emma?'

If she had detected any hint of condemnation in his question Emma would have lied without a qualm, but although his tone was intense there was no challenge, so she shrugged and admitted, 'I like them well enough. I just prefer not to clutter my life with them.'

He was watching her carefully, reading every controlled nuance of expression. 'I can understand why, in view of your ambitions. But surely not wanting children of your own doesn't mean that you should feel threatened by other people's?'

Emma's stomach began to roil. He was getting too close, far too close. 'What is this? A psychological profile? Are you doing some undercover work for your brother, trying to find out whether there's any devastating little character defect that might affect my ability to do my job?'

'I don't see the connection,' Frazer murmured. 'Interesting that you should get so nervous about your job when I mention the unrelated subject of children and yet remain unruffled when I mention embezzlement, which is surely a far more serious threat to your integrity...'

'Did you say embezzlement?' Charles leaned forward sharply from his position of prominence on Sir Clive's right hand.

'Just discussing a hypothetical situation, Charles,' soothed Emma. At the muffled cough of amusement beside her, she forgot herself so far as to kick Frazer under the table. The cough turned into a gasp as he dropped his napkin. As he bent to pick it up, Emma felt a warm caress up her slender calf, feathering the inside of her knee, a very sensitive part of her body. She flinched, her eyes clashing with Sheena's knowing ones across the table. Perhaps Steven's wife was an old hand at games of footsie under the table, or perhaps she just knew her uncle-in-law. Her smirk said it all, but instead of piping up with the kind of malicious remark that Emma had come to expect from her, she winked!

By the time Emma got to bed her head was whirling. After that first embarrassing glass of wine she had been careful to refuse all refills but she still felt as if she were drunk. Sheena being kind, Steven being nervous, Sir Clive being over-jovial and Lady Conway being cautious? What was going on? Of the family only Miriam and Michael and Julie and Chester had seemed unaffected by the strange atmosphere at dinner. And Frazer, of course, whose quiet needling of Emma had never stopped. Those five were the ones who were not directly involved with ConCorp. Was there a secret that she wasn't yet privy to? Perhaps Sir Clive would enlighten her tomorrow. She had finally been invited to have her 'fireside chat' just before lunch. Last, but not least, she reminded herself firmly. And she would have plenty of time, in the morning, to go over her proposals again before she presented them.

Or she would have had, if she hadn't slept in, thanks to her series of nocturnal visitors.

The first tap on her door came not long after she had turned off her light. She was lying in the darkness trying to fathom the possible source of the evening's tensions when she heard a faint scratching. Then the discreet tap.

Frazer Conway.

She couldn't imagine anyone else on the island who would have the nerve, not to mention the arrogance, to come creeping to her room and expect to be admitted. It had to be him. She smiled grimly in the blackness as he tapped again, wondering how long it would take his massive ego to realise that she wasn't going to answer. She imagined him standing there as the knowledge of his failure sank in. With his looks and sexy confidence she didn't think that he failed very often. What would he do? Find someone else? Go tapping on Trudy's door? Emma sat up, then forced herself to lie down again. Whatever he did, it was no business of hers.

The tap became a definite knock and Emma's whole body tensed. She remembered his outrageous boldness. He probably wouldn't care if he woke the whole wing trying to get into her room. He might not, but Emma would. Edward would love it and it would confirm Charles's opinion that women were emotionally reckless.

Flinging back the summer-weight duvet, Emma switched on the lamp and slipped into her silky robe. She took a deep breath before she unlocked the door, summoning her coldest expression of disdain. She opened the door half a body-width and focused her cutting gaze at about the right height. Nothing!

'Can we come in?'

Her eyes dropped. Hot embarrassment overwhelmed her. It wasn't Frazer Conway at all. What on earth had made her fevered imagination think it was? Her ego must be even more bloated than his!

'What do you want, Amy?' she asked wearily.

'Can we come in?'

'I thought we decided——'

'This is a 'mergency,' said Amy importantly. 'Jessie's toe is hurting.' She dragged her companion forward. 'Isn't it, Jessie?' She gave her cousin a nudge. Jessie removed her thumb from her mouth and sniffed dolefully. They all looked at the tiny plaster on the tip of her toe.

'She can't sleep, it's so bad. Can we come in with you?' said Amy again, screwing her eyes up in an attempt to look pathetic, and only managing to look cunning. 'If your daddy's here we'll be *real* quiet, won't we, Jess?'

Thumb back in her mouth, Jessie nodded.

'Of course he isn't here. And Marc is not my daddy, he works for me,' said Emma hurriedly, widening the door so they could see the innocent bed. Quickly Amy sidled in, pulling Jessie by her sprigged cotton nightie. Reluctantly Emma shut the door behind them.

'Have you got sunburn? Your face is all red. Mum puts calamine on me when I'm burnt,' said Amy kindly.

Emma held her hands to her hot cheeks, willing her self-inflicted humiliation to fade. 'I'm just hot. It's a very warm night. Isn't it rather late for you to be roaming about the house? Why don't you take Jessie to see her mother?'

'Aunt Julie gets puffy eyes if she has to get up in the night. Can I have a drink of water?' Without waiting for a reply, Amy trotted into the bathroom to help herself. Jessie, not taking her big eyes off Emma, moved crabwise to the bed and climbed on. She crawled up to the pillows and pulled the bedclothes up after her. The thumb, unnecessary for the manoeuvre, remained firmly in place.

Amy came out of the bathroom and got into bed beside Jessie. 'Maybe if you told us a story we'd get sleepy,' she said.

'Only a short one,' Emma temporised, knowing she wouldn't get to sleep very quickly herself even if she took the children back to their rooms right now. She would brood on her own shameful error.

Of course, one short story became one very long story, because Emma's intellect demanded a certain challenge in whatever she did. Amy was enthralled and Jessie's thumb fell out of her mouth as they wended their way through a vicarious adventure and Emma felt the familiar surge of pleasure that so frequently undermined her determination to keep children firmly at a safe distance.

She was somewhere in the middle of the tale when there was another knock at the door. This time she didn't allow herself any delusions. One look at Amy confirmed her suspicions. 'I wonder who that could be?' she murmured drily.

Amy picked at the sheet. 'Dunno.'

They didn't have to wait. Emma hadn't relocked the door and it was suddenly slammed open. Lizzie stood there, sausage curls on end, ubiquitous finger pointing triumphantly.

'Emma!' She looked around the room, no doubt for lurking daddies, and then nodded vigorously at James and the two other children crowded into the doorway. George and Teri, Amy's brother and sister, Emma guessed without effort. It appeared she was hosting a full complement of Lady Dorothy's grandchildren.

'Shhh!' said Jessica around her thumb.

'Emma's telling us a story. Get in the bed and listen,' ordered Amy.

George at nine and Teri at eight were more restrained than their younger relatives and actually hovered for a few seconds before they dived for the by-now jumbled bed. Emma noticed that James was carrying a lumpy pillowcase.

'What have you got there, James?'

'In c-case we g-get hungry,' he said, opening his burden to show her the contents.

'I'm hungry now,' said Amy, bouncing up to help herself to a fistful of chocolate biscuits.

'Not in my bed, you're not,' said Emma, trying to regain control of the situation.

'It's not midnight yet,' said George, looking at his robot watch. 'We can't have a midnight feast until midnight.'

'Let's *pretend* it's midnight,' said Teri, inspired.

In the end Emma spread a crumb-catching sheet on the floor by the window and they all clustered on it, stuffing themselves with an impressive menu filched earlier from the kitchen. Evidently a feast had always been on the cards, it was only the location which had come under heavy discussion, with Amy and Jessie sent ahead as scouts.

Emma refused to start the story all over again for the benefit of the larger audience, instead re-weaving the ending so that they all managed to play a part. Emma enjoyed their reactions so much that she lost track of time and was horrified to glance at her watch and see that it was nearly one a.m. There were cries of protest when she announced that the party was over. She lined them up in order of size and was about to march them back to their rooms when there was another tap at the door.

The children froze.

'I bet it's Horrendous Horace!' whispered George hoarsely, naming the evil villain of the story.

Lizzie gave a little squeak of terror that was cut off by Amy's ungentle hand over her mouth. 'No, it's probably Mum,' she said practically. 'Boy, is she gonna be mad about all that stuff James sneaked from the kitchen.'

'Y-you helped t-too,' accused James in childish outrage.

'Quiet, all of you!' said Emma. 'Let me see who it is, first.'

'Please don't tell on us.' said Teri urgently. 'We're not supposed to come over to this part of the house at night. It's one of Grandma's rules.'

The general holding of breath convinced Emma that Grandma's rules were obviously not lightly flouted. 'Let's wait and see who it is.' She had no intention of lying to their worried mothers.

In a concerted action the children scurried round behind the bed, out of the sight of the door, as Emma opened it cautiously.

'It's only me.'

Soft as melted honey, Frazer's words stole her breath away. Her earlier embarrassment returned in a rush. She blushed as his heavy-lidded eyes caressed her thin robe. 'I saw your light under the door,' he told her, still enjoying the view as he rested his shoulder against the rough-cast wall of the hall. 'Can't you sleep?'

Emma wedged her body in the narrowly open door, blocking his view of the room. 'You obviously haven't even tried.' He was still wearing his dinner suit, his jacket gaping, black tie loosened and his shirt rumpled out of the top of his trousers.

'Steven and I stayed up to...talk. Then I thought I'd come and say goodnight. You didn't say goodnight to me, Emma...you were tryin' to avoid me...'

His blue eyes were no longer vivid and sharp but soft, and slightly out of focus.

'You're drunk!' she realised.

He smiled. 'A little more than slightly. In fact, to tell the truth, a lot. But not utterly smashed, like Steven. Did I tell you how beautiful you looked tonight? But I like you better now, all mussed from your bed. Your hair doesn't look so pale when it's swimming across your shoulders like that. I'd like to dive into it, I'd like to see it spread across my pillow...or better still, across my skin——'

Acutely conscious of impressionable ears flapping behind her, Emma cut him off sharply. 'I have better things to do than stand here in the middle of the night and listen to the ramblings of a drunk. I suggest you go to bed and sleep it off.'

'Aren't you going to invite me in?' He showed her the half-bottle of brandy and two glasses clutched loosely in his hand. 'A nightcap might help you relax.'

'No!' She lowered her voice to an icy trickle. 'I am perfectly relaxed, Frazer, I don't need any help from you. Will you just *go away*.'

'What a cruel mistress you are. Steven was right...'

'Right about what?' She regretted the question as soon as it slipped out, even thought her interest was piqued. It would only give him the excuse to linger.

'That, given an inch, you have the potential to emasculate the entire board of directors...'

'Steven said that?' Emma stiffened. She had always thought that the liking and respect she had for Steven was mutual. Should she place any importance a conversation between two drunks? Did his comment mean that Steven didn't support her promotion? If he wasn't for her, that could only mean that he was against her...

Befuddled as he was, Frazer sensed his tactical error. 'He only said *potential*, honey. But then, he doesn't know you the way I know you. He doesn't know what you're like inside. He doesn't know you're all soft and sweet and womanly...'

For the second time in twenty-four hours his kiss took her by storm. This one was a lot less innocent than the first. His tongue traced the outline of her surprised mouth, flickering lightly inside to flavour her senses with

the heady taste of brandy and man. As he leaned into
her he staggered slightly and placed his free hand against
her breast to steady himself. Flame shot through Emma's
stunned senses. Frazer's fingers curled naturally around
the warm mound, tightening, and he made a rough sound
of content at the feel of her. 'Did I tell you how much
I love honey? I know I'm going to love you, honey, just
as much...'

From behind her in the room there came a muffled
but distinct giggle. Frazer lifted his mouth. 'What was
that?' he slurred lazily.

'Nothing.' Emma's voice failed at the first attempt and
she had to try again. Hurriedly she brushed his hand
from her tautening breast. 'Nothing.'

He looked at her flushed face, his brain slowly making
connections. 'Is there someone in there with you? Is that
why you won't let me in?' he asked with very careful
precision.

'No, of course not!' She didn't want him to confront
the children, or vice versa, in his maudlin state. 'You're
imagining things. It's all those brain cells you just an-
nihilated. You'll be seeing pink elephants next.'

Her scorn might have worked except there was
another, quickly stifled whisper from behind her.
Frazer's body tensed and suddenly took on a new and
dangerous lean.

'Is it Fletcher? Is that who you've got with you?'

Emma's damp hand kept tight hold of the door-handle
as she began to ease it imperceptibly closed. 'Just go
away, Frazer. We'll talk about it in the morning.'

'I want to talk about it now.'

'Well, I don't. You don't own me, Frazer. I'm not
answerable to you.'

He smiled a crookedly sardonic smile and she braced
herself for a fresh attack of belligerence, but it didn't
come. For some reason her words leashed his aggression,
although the hostility was still there in the hard jut of

the roughened jawline and the tight line around his mouth.

'You think not? Enjoy the delusion while you can, honey, because it's not going to last much longer.' He raised his voice. 'Hear that, Fletcher? Your days are numbered, pal. Tonight's your swansong, so you'd better make it memorable.' His voice dropped again to that first, liquid softness. 'From tomorrow, Emma, all your sleepless nights are going to be because of *me*...'

The statement had been delivered in something like the manner of a vow, and long after Emma had deemed it safe to shepherd her involuntary charges back to their rooms she worried over what had made him so certain.

At lunchtime on Sunday she was no longer worrying. She was totally numb!

Her interview with Sir Clive had gone well. He seemed to be very impressed with her ideas; he had invited her to call him Clive; he had talked about 'fresh blood' and 'shake-up' and 'change' in a way that led her to believe the future was all positive. When Emma went to lunch she was still soaring.

Sunday lunch was served in the tropical lushness of the conservatory where Lady Conway grew her prized orchids. Steven was wearing dark glasses, Emma was amused to note, and Frazer, looking decidedly seedy, avoided her assiduously, which was an immense relief. Perhaps he had polished off the rest of the brandy himself and suffered a memory black-out. She hoped so.

After they had eaten, Sir Clive rose to his feet, smiled affably at them all, and delivered his shattering bombshell.

Steven, he announced, had not been happy at ConCorp for some time but had hung on out of a sense of family duty. Now he felt the time had come for him to make the break and realise a long-held private dream—to establish himself as a craftsman of fine, handmade furniture. His skill at what had hitherto only been a hobby had already earned him a reputation at craft shows and galleries and now he wanted to give a full range of expression to his talent.

'Naturally it's a disappointment to me that my only son doesn't share my loyalty to the company which bears the family name and honour, but I accept that each man must live his life the way he sees fit...' It was the only hint of the ructions Steven's decision must have caused. Sir Clive wouldn't have given in without a fight. 'However, thankfully there is another member of the family who is willing to take up the burden of leadership. I refer, naturally, to my brother, Frazer, who has forsaken a very lucrative and successful international business of his own to come home and take over Steven's responsibilities at ConCorp...and, in the fullness of time, my own...'

Frazer Conway was to be the new head of ConCorp!

The knowledge sank like a lead weight into Emma's outraged consciousness.

Last night's drunk-at-the-door was going to be her new boss.

And it followed that the new boss would have a major say in who ConCorp's new Chief Executive would be.

That person would obviously not be Emma Rainer!

CHAPTER FOUR

FRAZER CONWAY watched the woman push through the glass doors of the restaurant and approach the *maître d'*.

She wore a navy double-breasted jacket, wide in the shoulders and long at the waist, over a cream and navy blouse with a self-scarf and tailored navy skirt. Her high-heeled cream shoes matched the slim leather satchel tucked under her arm. Her pale blonde hair was caught in some kind of complicated twist on the top of her head, the icing on top of the cake. He leaned back in his chair, amused at the whimsical thought, knowing that it would get a reception as frosty as her hair if he murmured it aloud. She was talking to the *maître d'*, obviously familiar with him, presenting her back to the room. He noticed the flirty little frill in the split at the back of her neat skirt, yet another of the tiny contradictions that studded her character like a fine haze of cracks over the glossy façade.

She turned, smiling at something the man had said. The smile sent a familiar jolt through his relaxed body. It was not surprising that she smiled so rarely in the office. The smile was breathtaking. It eclipsed the businesswoman and made her simply, and utterly, a woman. When her mouth tilted, the whole of her face went with it, moving into a series of soft, rounded, inviting curves, her big, honey-coloured eyes widening to reveal a shimmering clarity.

Her mouth was disproportionately large in the small face, the superficial reason for the nickname he had heard whispered around at ConCorp: the Mouth Trap.

If she knew about it she was probably flattered. It was as much a tribute to her steel-trap mind as to that distinctive mouth, an indication of the healthy respect, mixed occasionally with fear and envy, that she commanded in both colleagues and underlings alike. The mouth, when it wasn't smiling, could snap egos like dry twigs and the tongue could provide the blistering heat to consume the remains to ignominious ashes.

She was walking between the tables now, with a swinging, confident, to-hell-with-you stride that indicated some of the forcefulness in that small frame. Venus when she smiles, but Juno when she walks... the quotation flitted through his Frazer's mind as he watched her move, waiting for her to spot him. When she did he was ready for her reaction. The remains of her smile froze on her face, her body stiffened, but she never faltered in her stride. He admired her refusal to give him even that tiny victory. He had been in and out of ConCorp's head office for the past week, consulting with Clive and Steve, meeting various department heads, but so far Emma had succeeded in speaking to him only in passing on her way to yet another urgent appointment. They both knew that she was avoiding him, and they both also knew that, up until now, he had let her. Anticipation was as sweet on his part as it was probably sour on hers. Today was his first twitch on the reins. He had a private bet with himself that she would pull strongly, testing his strength, before she submitted to the inevitable. The lady was too proud to give in without a fight, but too ambitious not to know when it was politic to do so.

Emma could feel her breathing quicken as she approached the table, trying to keep her eyes fixed on Sir Clive's face, all the while aware of the other, unexpected and unwelcome, presence at the table. The awareness was constant, disturbing her normally aggressive self-confidence. Even just catching a glimpse of Frazer

Conway around the ConCorp building was enough to set her nerves jangling. When Marc had informed her of this late appointment for lunch with Sir Clive at a nearby restaurant she had been quietly buoyant. A decision at last? Since that shattering weekend there had been no progress on the Chief Executive appointment. Steven himself had told her why, while apologising to her for the necessity of keeping everyone in the dark about his plans and assuring her that he had indeed touted her to his father as the best choice for Chief Exec.

It appeared that, right up until that weekend, nothing had been settled about the ConCorp succession. Frazer Conway had *not* come back to New Zealand to take over, he had returned to establish a local engineering consultancy. In fact, for months he had been resisting Sir Clive's pleas that he run the family firm. But, settled or not, Steven had promised Sheena he would quit the business that he had come to resent, a resentment that had spilled over into their marriage, and was not about to withdraw his resignation. It was only on the Saturday night after dinner, Steven had revealed, that Frazer had suddenly, without explanation, changed his mind.

'It was a load off my mind, I can tell you,' he'd confided. 'God knows what finally convinced him. Dad had been using every inducement known to man and it made no difference. Frazer's always had a healthy contempt for power-broking as such. He's not exactly what you would call conventional in his thinking and he's always enjoyed the... *physicality* of being an engineer—actually getting out there and *doing* things as opposed to just planning it and delegating others to carry it out. Even as a consultant he gets involved in the nitty-gritty reality of his projects—that's what makes him so good. But I wasn't going to stare a gift horse in the mouth. I've wanted this chance for years and I wasn't going to let it slip through my fingers out of misguided concern for someone who can very well look after himself...'

Steven had suddenly grinned as he added, 'Just for good measure I got him smashed that night so he wouldn't have time to change his mind before Dad made his little speech. Or did he get me smashed? All I remember is, Sheena kicked me out of the bed and I had to sleep on the couch...'

'Sit down, sit down.' Sir Clive had risen, gesturing with his cigar, as Emma reached the table. She had no choice but to sit where he indicated, between the two men. Frazer, she noticed, didn't stand, and she gave him a haughty little nod as a waiter rushed over to draw out her chair.

'I thought you'd be offended,' he murmured.

'I beg your pardon?' she said, in a cool voice that told him she would never do any such thing.

'If I rose to your womanhood. I assumed you were above demanding such gestures to sexual inequality. I just wanted you to know that I was being thoughtful, rather than rude.'

'I didn't even notice,' she said in the same, cool, dismissive voice. How dared he attempt to read her mind? He grinned. Even his teeth were film-star perfect, strong, white and even. Probably capped, she thought snidely.

'Let's order, then we can get down to business.' Sir Clive didn't even look at the leather-bound menu. 'I'll have the usual, Wallace,' he told the waiter. 'Frazer, you'll have a steak, won't you? After all that Yank fuel-injected, corn-feed stuff it'll do you good to get your teeth into some *real* meat for a change, some good, pure Kiwi beef. Medium-well done, Wallace.'

'Make mine rare,' said Frazer equably, as the white-haired waiter began to scribble.

'Emma? Steak?' Sir Clive's bushy eyebrows drew together as he invited her to join them...to show she was as red-blooded a carnivore as any man.

'I'll have the John Dory,' she said, refusing the invitation. She had no need to prove herself through her stomach.

Sir Clive harrumphed and opened the wine list. 'I suppose red wine won't go with your fish.'

'Just order for yourselves, Sir Clive. I'll have iced water. I have a legal seminar this afternoon and I'd rather have a completely clear head.'

She earned herself another snapping stare. Sir Clive ordered a bottle of claret without consulting his brother and then led off with another challenge. 'I thought I told you to drop the "Sir".'

'Actually, you *asked* me,' said Emma. 'And if you remember I declined. It just wouldn't feel right.'

'Because I'm old enough to be your grandfather, I suppose,' he said gruffly.

'That and the fact that I think you *earned* your knighthood,' she admittedly calmly, knowing that Sir Clive used his gruff, bluff demeanour deliberately. If he could intimidate you, he would. Showing uncertainty was tantamount to waving a red rag at a bull. 'It's also a matter of respect for your position in relation to mine...'

He gave a barking laugh that showed admiration for her subtle probe. 'Trying to find out whether the relativity of our positions is going to change? Sorry, Emma, that's a decision that has to be made by a full board, and we don't have another meeting for three weeks.'

Emma was careful to keep her disbelief within bounds. Everyone knew that Sir Clive *was* the board.

'Does all this hearty respectfulness mean that I'm going to have to answer to "Mr Conway"?' murmured the man on her left, tired of being ignored.

'Respect has to be earned, *Frazer*,' she said sweetly, looking him in the eye for the first time.

'When I get my knighthood, will you call me sir?' he asked, blue eyes taunting.

'Among other things.'

Such was his command of her senses that she had momentarily forgotten Sir Clive. He chuckled, puffing his revolting cigar. Emma held her breath as a cloud of smoke drifted past and wished she had to courage to ask him to stub it out. But there were limits to her bravery.

Frazer leaned over and plucked the offending object from his brother's veined fingers and stubbing it out. 'You know what Dot has to say about smoking at the table... not to mention the fact that you're turning us green. They may like their steaks with the consistency of tissue paper in the States, but at least they provide you with clean air in which to enjoy it.'

'You smoke like a chimney yourself,' Sir Clive complained a trifle petulantly as Frazer signalled for the ashtray to be removed from the table.

'Used to, Clive, used to. Haven't you noticed I've given up? I'm disgustingly healthy these days. Now that my lungs are operating efficiently, my stamina and sense of physical well-being have increased dramatically...'

Looking at him sideways under her lashes, Emma had to agree that his health was indisputable. His light grey suit and pink shirt sheathed him beautifully, showing off that prime physique, and there was a healthy sheen to his tanned skin and glossy hair and eyes. He looked very fit and very... male.

'I suppose you want me to send the wine back, too,' Sir Clive grumbled.

'I'm not an extremist. I enjoy wine much more than I used to now that I don't strain it through tobacco. In fact, come to think of it, some of the most haunting memories in my life have been created after a few drinks to oil my creaking inhibitions...'

He was looking directly at Emma as he mused and she knew then that he had suffered no black-out after his island binge with Steven. He remembered everything, it was written in those blue, blue eyes. Emma felt an internal glow sweep through her body and she struggled not to allow it to the surface. She wouldn't remember the way his lips had stroked hers, the way he had tasted, the feel of those blunt, strong fingers moving on her breast...

'I didn't realise you had any,' she said severely, to stop herself dwelling on exactly what she wasn't going to let herself dwell on.

'Inhibitions?' The blue eyes glittered. 'I'm thirty-seven, honey—you don't get to my age without learning the value of restraint. Of course, I won't deny that I've lost an inhibition or two along the way as well as gaining a few, but not to the extent of practical immorality. Clive will vouch for the fact that for the last five years I've been a commendably model, if mobile, citizen.'

'You don't think I'd let him loose in my company if I didn't trust him.' Deprived of his cigar, Sir Clive was forced to stab in Emma's direction with his finger. 'I'd trust him with my life. Hell, I *am* trusting him with my life.'

'And he has the security checks to prove it,' said Frazer drily.

Emma was shocked. 'You mean you ran a security check on your own *brother*?' she asked Sir Clive.

He ignored her, glaring at Frazer. 'How did you know?'

'Because I ran one or two on you.' Frazer admitted calmly. 'Just wanted to make sure that your cries for help were legit. That you weren't prettying up the books to entice me back with the intention of blaming me for your, or Steven's, mistakes.'

Sir Clive spluttered. 'You ran checks on *me*? Why, you arrogant jackass. I've been a father to you. I brought you up from a snot-nosed kid. Where the hell do you get off doubting me? I'm the one who's responsible for all those fat dividends that helped put you on track with your bloody bridge-building. You think I would try and con *you*?' His voice rose in booming outrage, his complexion turning alarmingly red.

'Watch your blood-pressure, old man,' Frazer grinned, 'or you'll be retiring sooner than you expected. Not con exactly, no, but you wouldn't be above a little emotional blackmail. You can't fault me for wanting to know if there was anything you were glossing over, can you? What was your excuse?'

Sir Clive's mottled colour subsided a little and he barked a laugh. 'I thought you might be in some trouble, and that's why you wanted to come running home. You spent all those years building up that firm and you were suddenly going to hand it over to your partner and walk away. I thought he might have something on you.'

'You could have asked.'

'You'd probably have told me to mind my own business. You never did like asking for help.'

'I never needed to. It was constantly being thrust upon me. As it happens Andrew gave me a very good price for my half of Freeman Conway.'

'I know.' Sir Clive couldn't quite hide his smugness. But he couldn't quite leave it alone. 'Although I still think you could have beat him up a few points. Better still, you could have hung on to a piece. Doesn't hurt to hedge with US funds——'

'Maybe we can discuss this later. I'm sure we're boring Emma with our little family squabble,' said Frazer smoothly as their steaks and her fish arrived.

Actually Emma was fascinated. It was yet another insight into the complex Conway family relationships. Frazer seemed quite resigned, even amused, that Sir Clive should have secretly invaded his privacy, while his half-brother acted as much proud as outraged that the favour had been returned. It seemed that the Conways enjoyed Machiavellian manoeuvres and had no qualms about mixing business with personal motives. Emma, who had spent her entire professional life making sure that the two were carefully separated, felt as if she had suddenly stepped on shaky ground.

She was glad that she had ordered fish. The knot in her stomach didn't leave much room for food. She was doubly glad of her choice when Sir Clive suddenly said, 'The reason I asked you here, Emma, is that I want you to work with Frazer for the next few weeks. Take him around. Show him the ropes, that sort of thing.'

Emma nearly choked on a flaky piece of fish. 'But I thought Steven——'

'Oh, I know, Steven's been working with him, but his mind's not on the job, it's already on his damned furniture. So I told him if he wants to go he may as well go now. All Frazer needs for a few weeks is a temporary backstop, a guide, someone who knows all the ins and outs and who can discreetly stop him making a fool of himself if the occasion arises——'

'Thanks, Clive.'

Frazer was waved down. 'You know what I mean—you did it yourself for years. A consultant, that's what he needs, and you're the man, Emma.'

'He means that as a compliment,' said Frazer, with a straight face.

'I don't need you to translate, thank you,' said Emma, still in a mental turmoil. 'But, Sir Clive, I have a department to run. I can't just push it aside to act as nursemaid——'

A glower. 'Frazer's a big boy, I'm not asking you to wet-nurse him——'

'Pity,' murmured Frazer, eyes drifting down to her breasts, which heaved indignantly as she registered the significance of his regretful mockery.

Fortunately, Sir Clive didn't appear to notice the electric interchange of glances. 'He won't need you all the time——'

'That's a matter of opinion...'

Emma was fed up with the innuendo. 'If you can't contribute anything constructive to this conversation, Frazer, would you mind shutting up?' she snapped.

He folded his hands meekly in his lap, his eyes laughing at her as Sir Clive steam-rollered on. 'Just be on call if he does. There'll be meetings—contracts—he won't be familiar with yet. He'll soon pick it up. In the meantime Shriver can provide back-up for you; he's a competent young man, isn't he?'

'I hired him myself,' said Emma of her second-in-command.

'Well, then... Don't you think he's capable of holding the fort for a few hours a day?'

She was in a cleft stick. If she protested Sir Clive would think that she was afraid to delegate.

'You might even consider this as a dry run,' said Sir Clive with innocent cunning. 'Mind you, I'm not promising anything—as I say, that's up to the board. But the fact that Frazer asked for you and not one of the others, well, that's bound to give them a favourable impression...'

Emma ignored the carrot in favour of the stick. 'You *asked* for me?' she said hollowly, suspicion raising its ugly head.

Frazer was slicing into the last of his steak. He shrugged. 'It seemed like a good idea at the time,' he murmured.

'Why?'

'I just told you why,' interrupted Sir Clive testily. 'Well, I can't sit around here all day. No, don't hurry, Emma——' as she pushed her half-empty plate away '—you stay here and settle up with Frazer.' Emma's instinctive protest died on her lips as he barked, 'And no more of that false modesty, or I'll begin to think you don't have the self-confidence to handle promotion....'

Sir Clive barrelled his way out of the restaurant with his customary disregard for protocol, waving away the *maître d'* who rushed to open the door for him.

'You realise the miserly old devil's left us to settle the bill,' said Frazer drily, after a small silence, deftly pulling Emma's frustrated attention back to himself by asking with an innocence that matched his half-brother's, 'Have you got a credit card on you?'

'You want *me* to pay?' For some reason, even though she carried a ConCorp Gold Card, Emma was outraged. 'You were the one who arranged this little get together. *You* pay.'

'How about if we go Dutch?'

'This is not a date. Put it on your expense account.'

'As what?'

Her eyes began to kindle. 'I'm sure you'll think of something. You appear to be very...' she sought for an appropriate word to signal her suspicions, and chose one she instantly regretted '...inventive.'

His eyelids drooped, his hard mouth taking on a sexy tilt. 'So I've been told,' he said silkily, and she drew a swift, sharp breath as she imagined by whom and in what circumstances he had been so informed... She had to get a hold on herself!

'Look, if you think—if you imagine—don't think that manoeuvring me into this position entitles you to...' Her voice petered weakly out as his eyes sparkled with new devilry, slowly perusing her rigid posture in the high-backed chair. Emma snapped her knees together under the table, her teeth clenching against the forbidden notion that her innocent words had amounted to an indecent invitation. His look of wicked intrigue suggested as much, and making love on a narrow chair in a public restaurant would certainly demand his self-admitted inventiveness. Damn him, he was doing his best to make sure they could never work together!

'How dare you treat me like this?'

'Like what?' His eyes veiled their gleam behind a polite enquiry.

'Like...the way you spoke in front of your—Sir Clive. The way you looked at me...'

'As if I found you an intensely exciting, desirable woman?'

'I—yes—no!' she hissed at him, taking a surreptitious look around, to make sure there was no one else from the office within eavesdropping distance.

'But I do,' he said simply, leaning back in his chair, toying with the last of his wine. 'Would you have preferred me to have pretended I didn't notice?'

'Yes!' If people couldn't overhear them, they would certainly be able to see her furious confusion in her flushed face.

'Why? Are you ashamed of being a woman?'

She was instantly defensive. 'Of course not! I'm proud of being a woman.'

'Then why don't you act like it?'

'Being proud to be a woman doesn't mean that I have to accept unwanted advances from any Tom, Dick or Harry——'

'I agree. The essence of the matter being contained in that word "unwanted",' he said smoothly. 'I was merely paying you the compliment of being honest. But perhaps you're one of those irritating women who like to play coy games with men, or worse, who try to deny that two sexes even exist. I refuse to ignore the fact that you're a woman, Emma. If you find that a problem, I'm sorry, but the problem is yours rather than mine and you must handle it as best you can. Now, as to our agenda for the next few weeks...'

With breathtaking ease he switched to business, leaving Emma floundering in his wake as he listed his expectations and invited her input. He was treating her exactly the way she had always demanded to be treated, so why was it suddenly so difficult to respond with her usual professional calm?

For the next twenty minutes she received a pointed lesson in the dangers of losing one's objectivity. She had known, of course, that he was an extremely successful engineer, but her antagonism had temporarily blinded her to his abilities. The scales were now coolly ripped from her eyes. Frazer Conway demonstrated a disconcertingly quick and complex mind as he sketched his opinion of the strengths and strains he had observed in his short time at ConCorp. His intellectual breadth and grasp was a great deal more commanding than she would have expected, given the narrowness of his speciality. She was shocked to find that it was sometimes a struggle to keep up with his darting thoughts. Her pride was piqued. He managed to make her feel dull, pedantic...she, who was considered a radical in the ConCorp ranks for her forward-thinking ideas! Her resentment, inextricably linked to that damnable physical awareness, tightened a notch.

They had coffee, still talking, and lingered, bargaining over Emma's time, Frazer conceding that she required a certain number of hours to herself each day but making it crystal-clear that in a crunch he expected to be her first priority.

'If you have problems coping with the workload, we can reassess the situation. But bear in mind it's only temporary...'

Emma's pride flared immediately. 'I can cope,' she said with a touch of husky scorn creeping into her coolly modulated voice.

'I'm sure you can. I've heard that you're efficient to the point of ruthlessness.'

'Oh? What else have you heard?' She wondered whether Edward or Charles had found the time to whisper a few perfidies about her.

'Nothing that jars with my own assessment,' he said, matching her for casualness.

Her curiosity raged furiously, but her reply was amused, impersonal, disinterested... 'And what is that?'

'You can read it in my report to the board.' He signalled the waiter for the bill.

Her honey eyes congealed into amber resin. Oh, he was good. That open manner, that frank use of language, that teasing masculinity—it all combined to fool one into thinking he was totally up-front. But Frazer Conway, she was beginning to discover, had all the hallmarks of a Titanic-sized iceberg, chugging into her sights. What you saw was a great deal less substantial than what you eventually ploughed into!

He caught her look. 'Now, Emma, would you have me behave unprofessionally and give you an edge on the others just because I want to gain your favour?'

'Certainly not!' she snapped, denying that she had even fleetingly toyed with such an underhanded, tempting idea.

'Hard, isn't it?'

'What is?' When all else fails, play the dumb blonde!

'Trying to resist playing on the male-female tension between us. You don't have to fight it so hard, you know, Emma. I don't have any problems with the idea of combining business with pleasure....'

'You aren't a woman. It's always the woman who gets fired,' said Emma tightly, suddenly seeing a way to head him off. She took a sip of water. 'However, I'm glad you feel that way. Because Marc Fletcher and I... well, we're involved...' She smiled, coyly inspecting her plainly polished nails, failing to realise that coyness was the last thing she should have feigned. Frazer didn't doubt that, if she were telling the truth, she would have taken fierce pride in flinging the fact in his teeth. He had known instinctively, on their first meeting, that here was a strongly passionate woman capable of scorning the limitations of convention if they clashed with her own powerful needs.

'On the island you were most emphatic that you and he were strictly boss and secretary,' Frazer said, folding his credit card into the bill that the waiter had offered him on a silver tray. Not a Gold Card, noted Emma absently, but Platinum....

'I...it only happened since then.' She couldn't claim to have been lying at the time without impugning her own honour. 'We realised that we...that we were....'

'Meant for each other? Compatible? Lusting after one another? I trust it wasn't I who gave my rival the impetus to confess his secret desires. I should hate to feel that my rejection sent him rushing into your arms on the rebound...'

'What on *earth* do you mean?'

'Your lover. I believe that I had first call on his...er...affections.' Now it was his turn to inspect his fingernails as she stared at him, her mind spinning wildly. Surely he couldn't mean...? *Marc?*

'I would have thought that, in this day and age, he would feel morally obliged to inform you of the risks involved in a er...switch-hitting...partner——'

'Are you saying that Marc made a *pass* at you?' the breathy words were redolent of shock.

'Discretion forbids me to say...'

'Bull! You're lying! Marc would never do such a thing!' Emma declared wildly, hoping it was true. If he *had* she would kill him. She would *kill* him!

'A man can't always control his inclinations——'

'I'm not talking about that! I couldn't care less about his sexual preferences.' She dismissed the unimportant with devastatingly revealing impatience. 'I mean, Marc would never jeopardise my promotion for the sake of...of... Oh, this is ridiculous!' Her common sense reasserted itself, reminding her of his propensity for provocation. 'Marc is *not* a homosexual.'

'I didn't say he was——'

'Bisexual, then. I don't believe it. He has tons of girlfriends——'

'He's never made a pass at *you*.'

'That doesn't prove anything,' said Emma hotly, on firmer ground here. 'Just because he's not attracted to *me*, it doesn't mean he's not attracted to women. In fact he and Trudy are——' She stopped abruptly, staring at him.

'Oh, dear.' Frazer tsk-tsked with a sorrowful face. 'Poor Emma. Trapped in the lonely corner of a love triangle...no wonder you're edgy——'

'Oh, shut up! That was a lie, wasn't it? Marc never made a pass at you!' And she had fallen for it, like a ton of bricks.

'You know, for such a shrewd operator, you can be appallingly gullible, Emma,' he confirmed with an unrepentant grin. 'I thought your lie deserved one in return. I've noticed Marc and Trudy having intimate little huddles all over the building and I doubted that your pride would permit any lover to be so openly unfaithful. But I must admit I never expected you to fall in so deeply. I shudder to think what ravages a corporate shark could inflict on that small-town naïveté of yours——'

She bristled even more. 'What makes you think I come from a small town?'

Frazer tempered his amusement, studying her thoughtfully. 'It was just a turn of phrase, that's all,' he soothed. 'I was being ironic. You have such a glass-canyon sparkle about you that I have difficulty imagining you in any other environment.'

'Don't patronise me!' she snapped, recognising his smooth insincerity for what it was.

He threw up his hands. 'Sorry, I thought I was paying you the compliment you wanted to hear. From your touchiness I take it that you *are* from a small town... There's nothing wrong with small towns, Emma. Quite the reverse. I've lived in them for most of my life and I can tell you that they're the same all over the world—jungle, desert, rural paradise, the cultures and customs may be different but the people are the same. They're part of a tribe. They have a stake in each other's future. They're far more inter-dependent than the mobile populations in big, impersonal cities and that's their ultimate strength. When civilisation falls it's the close-knit communities that will survive the crash...'

'With that paean to the joys of rural living I'm surprised that you should want to live in a city like Auckland,' said Emma tartly, relieved that his remarks had wandered away from the question of her origins.

'My wants aren't the only ones that have to be considered. However, Auckland can offer me the best of both worlds. What is it—fifteen minutes' drive to get out into the country?'

'You've been away a while; it's half an hour, at least, these days,' said Emma drily.

'Besides, I'm not saying that it's impossible to have a close-knit community within a city. Look at my family—the Conways qualify as a small town in terms of population and they certainly have a mutual stake in the future of ConCorp. So...if it wasn't Fletcher in your room that last night at the island, who was it?'

The flow of his words had continued so smoothly that she had opened her mouth to reply before she realised that this was another well-concealed trap. She shot him a smug look and remained silent, but her silence lasted only as long as his patience.

'I'm glad to see that you keep your promises, Emma,' he said blandly. 'The integrity of my executives is very important to me...'

She bit her tongue to stop herself feeding him the line he was obviously dangling for.

'You might be gratified to know that you have the minor-league section of the Conway town vote firmly in your pocket. The best midnight feast the gang have had in years, so I understand.'

Emma closed her eyes. Someone had ratted!

'George.'

Emma opened her eyes. 'I beg your pardon?' she said haughtily.

'Miriam's son. Miriam thinks he has his first crush. He wrote an essay about you at school. Earned himself an A for his mid-term English review. First A he's ever got. The family are ecstatic.'

Emma closed her eyes again. 'Oh, God...'

'I especially liked the pillow fight——'

Emma's head drooped into her hand. 'Oh, God...'

'And the part where you put the sheepskin rug over your back and moussed your hair into a unicorn's horn and charged at Horrendous Horace. I thought you looked a bit dishevelled when you answered the door.' He leaned across the table to murmur into her reddening ear. 'I'm afraid George has you pegged as a bona fide, certified *darling*. Miriam thinks the more humorous bits were made up but I had a chat with the boy, just to familiarise him with the laws of libel, you understand, and he swears it all happened. And, funny thing, all the other little witnesses corroborate his story.' Emma's head jerked up, infuriated to learn that he had been interrogating the children about her. Frazer met her speaking look with one of intimate collusion. 'Miriam says she's going to ask you round to dinner one evening and she's bound to mention the latest triumph among the offspring... Are you going to make a liar out of the boy, Emma, just for the sake of preserving your image as the stainless-steel corporate robot? Surely you couldn't shatter a young man's heart...not to mention his dreams...'

'Of course I wouldn't,' said Emma sharply, hoping that the contents of the essay hadn't reached Sir Clive's ears. 'George is a very pleasant boy——'

'I wasn't talking about George, I was talking about me.'

Emma stared stonily into the outrageous blue eyes.

'You don't just like children, do you, Emma? You *love* them, and they love you back. It's not a conscious effort, it's just the extension of a natural empathy. They sense that you're not going to judge or condescend, you let them set the pace and that's something that adults rarely do. What I don't understand is why you go to such pains to pretend otherwise. What are you afraid of? Or, rather, who made you afraid?'

'Are we finished with our business discussion? Because if we are I have things to do. Far more important things than sitting here and listening to your amateur psychoanalysis. Our relationship is purely business. You may enjoy mixing business with pleasure. *I* think it's fatal.'

And with that uncompromising announcement she stood.

'That's very admirable, Emma, but I think that you'll find it's rather unrealistic in the circumstances.'

'What circumstances?' Emma was driven to ask warily.

'Me.' He signed the credit-card slip with a flourish and stood, his blond head effortlessly lording it over hers. 'I'm very interested in you, Emma, in a very personal way, and I think the feeling is mutual or you wouldn't have needed to play the Fletcher Defence. I'll play your rules in the office by sticking to business when there's business to be done. But beyond that I reserve the right to make the most of my opportunities.'

'Be my guest. Just don't expect it to get you anywhere,' said Emma with a chilly contempt that didn't quite cover the tremor of huskiness that fringed her arctic tone.

He grinned. 'Persistence is my middle name. There's an old saying that I picked up somewhere in my travels:

"Women sometimes forgive those who force an opportunity... never those who miss it." You may have plenty of ammunition, honey, but you're going to find out that I have all the big guns!'

CHAPTER FIVE

'EMMA, I have a young gentleman here asking to see you.'

Emma impatiently depressed the button on her intercom as she checked her appointment book. 'Mr Grayson? Send him in.'

'Er, no, Grayson isn't here yet.'

Emma frowned. 'You know I can't possibly fit anyone else in without an appointment, Marc. I'm snowed under as it is.' She was surprised that he would even ask, and over the intercom, so that she had to edit her impatience in case the visitor was listening. She realised that her absences from the office over the past few days had put extra pressure on to Marc, but so far he had coped with no less than his usual skill.

'This guy I think you might make an exception for. He's family...'

The hint of amusement in Marc's voice had already tipped her off that it wasn't strictly business. Was it one of her brothers? They rarely travelled to Auckland, and when they did they always visited her at home rather than the office, but she didn't know of any other male relative who'd feel comfortable arriving unannounced.

Emma sighed. Brother or not, he would have to stand in line if he wanted more than a few minutes of her attention. The few hours to herself that she had negotiated with Frazer were crammed to the brim, not only with drafts and contracts that needed her approval, but with research on the company. She thought she had known all she needed to know about ConCorp, but it had only taken a couple of days at Frazer's beck and call to disabuse her. She hated it when he asked her a question she couldn't answer. It made her feel inadequate, even though he never indicated that he thought she was less than completely efficient because she didn't know everything. So she had spent every spare moment delving into old files and updating herself on current ones that normally didn't fall anywhere near her jurisdiction. At least it kept her head down, well out of Edward's way. He had been furious on learning about her temporary assignment and devoted himself to subtly making it as difficult as possible by funnelling a lot of unnecessary extra legal work to her department. So far she had kept the lid on her temper, but sooner or later she knew that she was going to blow. Before she did, she wanted to consolidate her position with Frazer.

Consolidate what position? Some time she must take a few moments to ponder the question. The past week had been tense and unsatisfactory. She had been braced for an unpleasant confrontation with Frazer over his arrogant assumption that she was available for a little action on the side. She had thought up all sorts of ego-slicing put-downs. It had replaced late-night TV as her favourite leisure occupation. And he hadn't given her an opportunity to use a single one of them! She was beginning to think that his behaviour must just have been some kind of executive obstacle course, a typically Machiavellian Conway manoeuvre to test her mettle. She should be pleased to have passed the test with flying colours by rejecting the offer to sleep her way to the top, but instead she was frustrated. She had looked forward to taking him down a peg or two.

At least, though, her awareness of him as a man had settled down to a manageable level now that he had stopped treating her like a woman. For all the notice he had been taking of her during their round of conferences and meetings, she might just as well have been a computer terminal programmed to spew out data at the punch of a key...and she grudgingly had to admit that Frazer certainly knew the right keys to punch. Steven might have been right that his uncle found no personal satisfaction in wielding power—Emma had noticed a certain bored restlessness in the blue eyes at times when one would expect him to be in a state of adrenalin-charged intensity—but he certainly was not intimidated by it. Quite the reverse. It was his very casualness in grasping the reins at ConCorp that intimidated everyone else. He made it look easy and they all knew damned well that it wasn't!

The door of her office opened and she began to rise, pinning on a smile. If she let her brother see that she was less than ecstatic he would take it as a confirmation of what everyone in Tirau had known since the day she had got on the bus to go to university: Emma would never be happy in the big city. She didn't belong there. One day, when she got over her fancy dreams of a big-time career and realised where she really belonged, she would come home and resume her real life. She got the lecture every time a member of the family came to visit, plus a list of the eligible bachelors of Tirau just panting for a good wife. Emma's legendary domestic reputation, it appeared, had not been dimmed by her years away in the evil clutches of the city. It had been kept alive by the confident expectation of her family that, any day now, she would want to fulfil her destiny with a good Kiwi country bloke!

But the figure in the doorway was not a six-foot, brawny farmer. It was not even four feet.

'Hello, Mzzzz Rainer.' Hands behind his back, the small boy carefully closed the door and advanced purposefully towards her desk. She knew he was a boy because he was wearing a suit, otherwise his prettiness would have misled her. A suit, on a child who hardly reached the top of her desk! His head was covered in beautiful golden curls and his face was in the process of losing its baby chubbiness, but not the glorious dimples that dented his cheeks as his rose-bud mouth smiled at her, his blue eyes slanting into mischievous squints.

'Hello,' she said faintly, sinking back in her padded chair. He wore a soft yellow shirt with the dark blue suit and a smart little blue bow-tie that matched his eyes. The colours should have clashed appallingly but somehow they didn't. He looked like the perfect mini-executive, if a slightly off-beat one. Emma's mouth twitched to control her grin, knowing that children were as entitled to their dignity as adults. For some reason this one didn't make her hackles rise defensively. Her voice lapsed back into the warm, natural husk that she had spent years ruthlessly refining to a cool, authoritative drawl. 'I suppose you're here after a job, young man. What sort of qualifications do you have?'

'I brought you these, Mzzzz Rainer.' His hand came from behind his back, clutching a little posy of tattered violets which he laid on the desk.

'Oh.' Speculation as to his identity was skewered by a shaft of delight. Pots of African violets on her kitchen window-sill were her sole concession to the occasional craving for the big, rambling, flower-filled garden that was her mother's pride and joy. Emma didn't have much of a green thumb herself, but she loved the freshness and colours of nature. Violets were a particular favourite.

'Hope you like them, Mzzzz Rainer.'

Emma looked around. 'Is there a bee in here?'

He laughed. Not a childish giggle. A laugh. Emma looked at him with raised brows. Who did he remind her of? 'Some women don't like to be called Mrs or Miss,' he said.

Emma's eyes glowed with approval. Whoever was bringing up the boy was doing a fine job. Someone had taught him to say 'women' instead of 'ladies' or 'girls', too fine a distinction for one so young to understand, but as an automatic response it would stand him in good stead later on.

'Well, I'm not married, and I don't mind if people call me Miss, but you can call me Emma,' she said. 'What shall I call you?'

She half expected, given the suit and the impeccable manner, for him to do it pompously, but he said, 'Tommy.'

'Well, Tom,' she thought the shortened form suited him better than the babyish one, 'I just love violets.' She picked them up and brushed the velvety petals across her cheek. 'They're small and sweet and adorable...' she couldn't resist adding teasingly '...just like you.'

He didn't blush but his blue eyes darkened. 'Boys can't be beautiful,' he said sternly, the faintest of lisps undermining his masculine authority.

Uh-oh, his feminist mentor had slipped up there. 'I meant handsome. If you want it, the job's yours. Any man who brings flowers to a job interview has got to have something going for him, even if it's only bare-faced bribery.'

'I don't want a job. I'm not old enough to work. What's bribery?'

She wondered whether it was wise to add the danger-ous word to his vocabulary. 'How old are you, Tom?'

'Five.' He looked at her slyly, to see how she was taking it. Her scepticism showed so he calmly readjusted to the truth. '*Nearly* five. Most people think I'm five 'cos I'm so pre-co-shus. That means clever.' No false modesty there. Who *did* he remind her of?

'Bribery is when you offer someone something they want in exchange for their doing something *you* want.' That sounded a little too innocuous. 'It's usually illegal or dishonest.'

'Like blackmail.' The curly head nodded understand-ingly. 'That's when you make someone do something they don't want to. Like when you make a kid tidy his toys away or you'll tell his dad that he wet the cat.'

'How could you wet a cat?' asked Emma, intrigued by his brooding air.

'By putting it in the fountain. It could touch the bottom,' he added quickly, when he saw her flicker of disapproval. 'And, anyway, it wanted to go in to eat the goldfish.' His voice rose in unconscious imitation of someone of higher authority. 'It needed to be taught a lesson.'

'Mmmm.' A touch of the incipient autocrat there. 'Well, Tom, it's been very nice of you to visit. But I have a lot of work to get on with——'

'I know. You're a *very* busy woman.'

For an instant Emma thought he was being sarcastic, but then she dismissed it as being ridiculous. A child of four wasn't capable of sarcasm. A niggle started at the back of her brain. She frowned. 'Why are you here, Tom?'

'To see if you can help me find a home.'

Emma blinked. 'I beg your pardon?'

'Somewhere to live.'

'Haven't you got a home?' she asked, startled.

He shook his head, golden curls bobbing. 'I want a big one. With a garden and a trampoline and a swimming-pool.' The big blue eyes looked at her so expectantly that Emma actually believed he thought she could produce one out of her desk drawer. The idea of having to disillusion him was strangely distasteful.

'Why do you think I can help you?'

His answer was a smile. Cute, toothy, adorable...and practised. He shot a yellow cuff, and leaned an elbow on the desk, then propped his face on his hand, thumping one foot over the other in a parody of every sexy office Lothario that Emma had ever seen. The niggle became a steady chomp as her eyes dropped to where the other dimpled little hand nudged the violets on her desk, reminding her who had brought them and how it had pleased her. She looked up. His eyes demanded to know how she could refuse such a personable little chap. No, not chap—a shark. A smooth-talking, miniature shark in a suit!

Emma was charmed. She grinned at him, letting him see that she saw through the con. He grinned winningly back. Like all good con-men he had an over-abundance of confidence. He would get to her in the end... My *God*! She suddenly knew who he reminded her of!

'Tom—what's your name, your *full* name?'

'Thomas Clive Conway.'

'My son.' The warm, gravelly pride in the deep voice came as much as a shock as his presence. Emma hadn't even noticed the door open.

Hell! was her first reaction as she had jolted to her feet. She had responded naturally to the boy, it would be cruel to revert to coldness now.

He was *married*! was her second, searing thought. 'Your *son*?' A bitter taste flooded her mouth as she glared accusingly at Frazer Conway. Not in a thousand, million years had she imagined him married. And with a child! How dared he shatter her preconceptions? Frazer and domesticity simply did not jell, not at *all*. 'Tom is *your* son?' she asked, just to make totally sure that her outrage was justified.

'For my sins.' He laid a hand on his heart.

'I bet there were a lot of those,' said Emma acidly.

'I think Emma's too busy to help us look for a house,' said Tom, straightening up, adjusting his suit as he walked over to his father. Their suits matched, noticed Emma incredulously. Father and son tailoring, for goodness' sake! It was crass, it was cute, it was...oh, God, it was disarming!

'Are you sure you asked her nicely enough?' Frazer enquired of his son. His *son*.

Tom frowned. 'I don't think I *said* please, but I meant it. Like Emma didn't really say thank you for the flowers, but I knew that was what she meant. Her eyes went all sort of goldy and her face went pink. She didn't hug me, though,' he added with a faint air of satisfaction that hinted at the discovery that his irresistible, dimpled charm could be a mixed blessing! Emma empathised with mixed blessings.

Empathising with the son, however, did not make her any more sympathetic towards the father. 'You sent him in here,' she realised.

'He wanted to come. He wanted to meet you.'

'And what about your wife? Does she want to meet me too?' asked Emma with seething sweetness.

'I only wish she could. Sally died four years ago in an air crash,' he said evenly. 'Tom's been staying at my brother-in-law's for a few weeks while I arranged things here. Andrew flew out with him before going on to Perth and Dubai.'

Emma felt a hot wave of shame wash over her. 'I...I'm sorry,' she stumbled, switching her gaze to the boy. 'I'm very sorry, Tom.'

'That's all right, Emma.' He heaved a sigh. 'If I had a mother we wouldn't need anyone to help us find the right house.'

Emma's aghast eyes shot up to Frazer's. He was waiting, smiling, which was another shock. 'He's not quite the callous little swine that he sounds, Emma. To him Sally's just the photograph of a pretty woman and a faint memory. And he's right. If she were here she wouldn't dream of letting me or anyone else choose the home she was going to live in,' his gaze kindled, 'much less a woman like you. I loved my wife but I've had four very intensive years——' this was a wry look at his charming shadow '—to get over the loss.'

She didn't know how to take that. Or rather she did, but refused the offer. What did he mean 'a woman like you'? 'Choosing a house is a very individual thing. I'm sure you don't want a stranger doing it for you——'

'I don't think of you as a stranger, and I trust your taste implicitly...' He cast a look over her beautifully tailored dress which contrasted the prim contradiction of cream collar and cuffs with the sensuous colour of a fine aged ruby wine.

'I couldn't possibly take the time——'

'We're in no hurry, are we, Tommy? There's plenty of room at Dot and Clive's, but I want to get us settled before Tommy starts school. That gives us a couple of months to look around. You don't have to feel under pressure, Emma. We'll take it as slow as you'd like... as slow as I can bear...'

Emma put her ringless hands flat on the desk in front of her, her mouth thinning. She was *not* going to get involved. Tom tilted his head against his father's hip and a large, slightly callused hand curled possessively over the little shoulder. In spite of the sophisticated clothes, in spite of the fact that she knew that Frazer Conway was an extremely wealthy and powerful man, there was something waif-like in the pose of man and boy. The two of them against the cruel, uncaring world. Emma was outraged by a sudden, treacherous surge of protectiveness in her breast. Those two needed protecting as... as she needed a good Kiwi bloke to settle down and have babies with!

'I'm sorry,' she said firmly. 'Since this doesn't come under the heading of company business I don't see the necessity of my becoming involved. A good real-estate agent is what you need—— '

'So now you're suggesting a stranger *would* be best?' Frazer's brow wrinkled in mock puzzlement.

Emma clenched her teeth. 'Well, I——'

'Don't you want to help us, Emma?' Tom asked curiously.

Emma had been brushing off childish demands for years, and from more deserving tots than this one. What made her will turn to mush at the sight of that calculating dimple? She knew very well that she was being blatantly manipulated.

'I think she's afraid of us, old chap,' his father answered for her.

'Afraid? *Emma?*' Tom looked shocked, as if his father had suddenly suggested that Wonder Woman might be a wimp. What on earth had Frazer been telling him about her? 'What is there to be afraid of?'

'Emma will explain. Tell him how you're afraid you might succumb to our fatal charm, Emma.'

'Don't talk such nonsense! Of course I'm not afraid!' She reacted badly, childishly, to the deliberate provocation.

'You're the one talking nonsense, Emma. It's not going to contaminate you to spend a few spare hours in my company. What if I promise that Tommy will always be with us? After all, he has a say in this, too. What can possibly happen with a four-year-old chaperon in attendance?'

Exactly what was happening now. Frazer's eyes and that slow smile and honey-smooth tone were saying things to her that not even a highly precocious four-year-old would understand, let alone have the presence of mind to object to.

'Surely Lady Conway——'

'Dot is a darling, but she and I don't see eye to eye on the subject of architecture.' Frazer put aside his son and moved in for the kill, circling around behind the desk. 'My family is well-meaning but inclined to enjoy interfering and I didn't come back in order to surrender my independence. We need you, Emma. Do you think I would have sunk my pride to come in here and beg a woman who I knew would take the greatest pleasure in knocking me back, if it weren't a matter of the greatest importance to me? Tom's spent all his life in America, he's bound to suffer a bit of a culture shock, he has to adjust to a new environment, make new friends and endure the curiosity and rather overwhelming attention of a big family of strangers. Then there's school to face——'

'Stop trying to convince me you're helpless,' she said shakily, in a low voice that wouldn't reach the child. 'I've seen you in action, remember. If you can step in cold and run a company like ConCorp you can certainly manage to organise your own household——'

'Ah, but I wouldn't be able to run the company without a team of experienced assistants like you to rely on. And I do know I can rely on you, Emma. Whatever you choose to tackle, you do it with the utmost determination. And at least I can trust you not to string out the task with the hope of insinuating yourself into my good graces . . . or do I mean my bad ones? Some women I know—not you, of course, Emma—would take advantage, would assume that this was an open invitation that I was hunting for a new wife as well as a new home, would use the opportunity to try and show what great nest-builders they are——'

Emma snorted and he kindly pandered to her contempt.

'But you're too shrewd to fall into that trap. After all, you know what a rakehell I am. You have first-hand experience. It's amazing I married at all, let alone happily. If I assure you I'm not harbouring any honourable intentions towards you, and you're free to continue to utterly mistrust and dislike me, will that help you feel more secure?'

Emma could feel herself going down for the third time. He was pin-pointing her objections, but double-Dutched into a contradictory jumble that, ominously, made a crazy kind of sense. As long as she kept her wits about her and expected the worst from him she would be safely armed against it. She would go about finding him a house with her usual efficiency and be shot of him in a week *and* have him nicely in her debt. Why not *really* give Edward something to get het up about...?

'I suppose I could find some time to——' she began weakly.

'Good! We can start this Saturday. I have a preliminary list from the real estate people that we need to weed down to possibles.' Frazer was brisk and resisted the urge to gloat.

His satisfaction, however, came through loud and clear. 'I was going to catch up on some work at home this weekend...' She must make it clear from the outset that her agreement didn't give him the right to expect rather than ask...

'Fine,' agreed Frazer smoothly. 'Tommy and I can come over early and help so that you'll have more time for us. We'll get through it in no time. How much mess can one highly motivated female executive create?'

'Perhaps I'll leaving the cleaning until Sunday,' said Emma hurriedly. The last thing she wanted was Frazer poking his nose around her possessions, enquiring as to why she needed to vacuum her bed. Home was sanctuary. She wasn't about to let his insidious influence creep into her personal life as pervasively as it seemed to have at the office.

He grinned and she felt an urge to kick him in the shins. he found her wariness amusing, because he confidently expected to overcome it. He had a lot to learn about Emma Rainer!

'We go to church on Sunday, with Aunt and Uncle,' said Tom, coming forward into the challenging silence.

'Oh, really,' said Emma faintly, disconcerted all over again, trying to envisage Frazer in a church pew.

'One must set an example,' said Frazer piously, a wicked gleam in his eye taunting her surprise. 'And where would a sinner like me get a warmer welcome?'

A small, leaping flame in the brown eyes gave him a brief hint of exactly where she thought he should go, but her reply, censored for the sake of the child, was forestalled by the sound of Marc on the intercom.

'Emma, Mr Grayson is here.'

'My eleven o'clock appointment,' she said with some relief, telling Marc to ask him to wait a few moments.

'Well, I suppose Tommy and I had better be on our way.' Frazer ruffled his son's hair. 'I'm showing him over the building and then I'm taking him to lunch. I don't suppose you're free to join us, Emma——?'

As a bird. 'No!'

'Ah.' There was a little silence and Emma cleared her throat looking for a neutral subject to see them politely out of the door.

'Where's your Dad taking you, Tom? Somewhere impressive by the look of that suit.' She couldn't help looking sideways at the full-sized original. To her reluctant amusement Frazer moved his shoulders sheepishly.

'He wanted to look like me,' he murmured with a touch of defensive aggression, 'and why shouldn't I indulge him? I can afford it.' His haughty eyebrows warned her not to make any smart remarks.

'You both look very cute,' said Emma, determined not to let him see how endearing she found him at that moment. 'The bow-tie particularly suits you.' She flaunted her defiance of his warning with a sweet sense of revenge. 'But shouldn't it have polka dots on it, or flashing lights, or something?'

Fortunately Tom stepped into the dangerous breach. 'We're going to a restaurant that serves hamburgers and steaks.'

'Let me guess, the steak is for you and the hamburger's for your dad,' Emma teased, her mouth curving into a wide, tender smile that few of her colleagues ever saw.

'How did you know my dad likes hamburgers?' Tom deadpanned, and Emma had to laugh.

'Four going on forty,' murmured Frazer, a little disgruntled that his son could make her laugh so easily whereas all he got was the cold shoulder. 'He's so sophisticated he terrifies me sometimes. He'll be cutting me out with women next.'

'He already has,' said Emma drily, moving pointedly around him to take his son by the hand and walk him over to the office door. 'It was lovely to meet you, Tom. I look forward to seeing you again on Saturday.' Strangely, she found it was the truth. Frazer Conway had already accurately guessed part of the reason for her wariness with children, so there was no point in pretending awkwardness with his son. Besides, it was difficult to imagine anyone not liking Tom, and at least a little boy was no threat to her peace of mind. It was the father, not the son, whom she had to beware of.

Tom held out his hand and Emma shook it gravely. 'You have a nice office,' he said tentatively.

'Thank you, Tom,' she said warmly. 'I chose the colour scheme and furniture myself.'

'I could maybe come back another time…when you're not busy,' he said carefully, with none of his former insouciance.

'Maybe you could,' Emma temporised.

'I wouldn't want to be a bother.' His politeness was more than a mere formality, and contrasted sharply with the eagerness with which children usually responded to her diffidence. Emma was stricken. Suddenly she saw beneath the charming sprite to the quiet kernel of puzzlement that touched him with anxieties beyond his years. He could hardly remember his mother but he must feel that there was something incomplete in his otherwise secure little world, something that having an indulgent father and being adorable and amusing and clever still couldn't quiet make up for. Impulsively Emma crouched down and cupped his little face.

'Friends are never a bother,' she told him gently. 'They can be irritating or infuriating or boring or stupid sometimes, but never a bother. A friend in need is a friend indeed.'

'What does that mean?'

That would teach her to resort to truisms. 'It means that if you ever really need me I'll make time for you,' she promised quietly.

His wistfulness lingered for an instant. 'Because we're friends?'

'Friends,' she confirmed, standing again. 'Now buzz off, friend, because I have work to do.'

'OK!' With an exuberance that burst the confines of his neat appearance, Tom flung back the door and scampered cheerfully into the outer office.

'That's some promise to make to a child. I hope you never let him down,' said Frazer evenly, to hide the blaze of triumphant emotion inside. Emma didn't realise it, but with that impulsive gift of herself to his son she had utterly sealed her fate.

'Of course I won't.' Emma's chin lifted. It was too late to regret her action.

'Good.' He was beside her again now, too close for comfort, but pride prevented her from stepping back. 'Because I love that boy. He's my heart and my soul, and what touches him touches me.' He lifted a hand and ran a finger along the underside of her proud jaw. 'What's part of him is part of me. That promise makes me your friend, too, Emma. And I take the demands and responsibilities of friendship *very* seriously.'

The pressure of the slightly callused pad of his fingertip tilted her face up and his mouth came down, warmly covering hers.

He tasted different. No alcohol this time, diluting the flavour of him, just pure essence of male. One arm went around her, supporting her against the hard length of his body while his mouth thoroughly explored her shocked lack of resistance. The measured, erotic thrust of his tongue into the moist sensitivity of her mouth was calculated to curl her toes. Emma began to struggle and was devastated by the easy strength with which he controlled her half-hearted protest. She felt his hunger in the strong fingers cupping her back, the thud of his heart vibrating against her breasts, the restless surge of his hard thigh against the constricting narrowness of the skirt that prevented him from tucking himself between her legs. He lifted his mouth and she dragged in a ragged breath, finding no will to object, and then he was kissing her again, harder, deeper, more intensely than before, taking her acquiescence for granted. A hand smoothed her buttocks through the linen fabric of her suit, adjusting her to fit his rising heat, while the other flattened out between her shoulder-blades, massaging her to his chest. The blood roared in Emma's ears and little black spots danced in front of her eyes. She thought she was going to faint as he plunged deeper and deeper into her mouth, feasting on her, filling her, sending a series of racking tremors shuddering through her body. Reality slipped into a surrealistic world controlled by sensation building upon sensation.

'Frazer, no ... you can't do this ...' she gasped when his mouth released her to find the taut arch of her throat. 'Not in my office, for heaven's sake——!'

'I'm glad you made that qualification,' he growled, his arms tightening momentarily, wedding them together for a long, breathless moment as he struggled to leash the passion that had flared so startlingly out of control. He had known that she aroused him, he just hadn't realised how vulnerable that made him, until this moment. With a sigh he put her firmly away from him, trying to ignore the provocation of that big, beautiful, kissable mouth. Her feeble protest seemed to have drained her of speech and he felt a hot, sinful pleasure at the knowledge that he had the power to still that clever brain, to reach past the fearsome logic to the passionate woman that nestled at the heart and soul of her being.

'Sorry, honey, I got a bit carried away,' he said huskily, the sweet taste of her still stinging on his lips. He rubbed his chest to ease the tightness there. 'Next time, how about exercising a little of your prerogative——?'

'*My*——?' Was he accusing *her* of having any control whatsoever over the situation? 'I had nothing to do with it!'

'No? I didn't go up in flames all by myself,' he told her with shattering certainty. 'I had some help. You didn't have to kiss me back. You're perfectly capable of making your own wants and desires known. You could have stumped one of your lethal heels on my foot, you could have bitten me. If you'd *really* wanted to stop me you could have turned me off like a tap. I may be crazy for you, but I'm not an animal. I'm aroused by response, not resistance.'

He was right, of course. It was futile excusing herself on the grounds of his greater physical strength. Her struggles had been less than convincing to either of them. She had been curious and had had her curiosity very thoroughly satisfied.

She licked her lips and he gave a rather explicit moan that made her colour bloom afresh, especially when she saw, over his shoulder, the very interested and amused faces of her secretary and her next appointment. The open door had given them a spectacular view of the proceedings within.

'Get out of my office,' she ordered fiercely, this time managing to be completely convincing.

'Yes, ma'am.' Frazer snapped a salute and left, collecting his son on the way, ignoring the two men in the outer office.

Emma watched them go, wondering gloomily how she was going to persuade Stuart Grayson to keep his mouth shut. He worked for one of Auckland's most prestigious legal firms, the one that handled all of ConCorp's conveyancing business, and was on gossiping terms with all of ConCorp's executive staff.

Somehow she was going to have to make that kiss a matter of client-lawyer privilege. Either that or accept a date. Stuart had been after one for months—a bet of some kind, she suspected. And by the triumphant gleam in his eye bribery was definitely a prospect!

CHAPTER SIX

'THE ceilings are too high.'

If Emma had been the type of woman to stamp her foot she would have stamped it right then. She settled for planting her feet firmly and folding her arms across her chest

'There is nothing wrong with the ceilings, or with the house for that matter,' she said tersely. 'The house you're looking for, the perfect house, does not exist. You have to settle for what you can get.'

'I'm sure I can get better than this.' Frazer leaned over to rap on the wall, tilting his head at the hollow sound.

'Don't tell me: dry rot,' said Emma sarcastically.

'Bad acoustics. A cough in the bedroom and you can hear it in the nursery.'

'Then you'll have to make sure you don't catch cold,' said Emma sourly. She doubted that coughing was what he meant. He was afraid that Tom might hear him in the throes of passion. Frazer would be a noisy lover, as uninhibited sexually as he was mentally. She could picture him in bed, that long, lean, tanned body flexing over a woman, enjoying her, urging her on, shouting out his sizzling physical pleasure in words that heightened the exquisite eroticism of the act...

'Emma? Are you all right?'

Her eyes jerked open and she stared at him in flustered horror. She had done it again. Drifted off in some adolescent sexual fantasy while Frazer rambled on about something totally prosaic.

'Of course I am,' she snapped guiltily. 'I was just thinking——'

'About what? It must have been something un-pleasant, judging from your pained expression.'

'It was,' she lied grimly. It was his fault she was going insane. He was impossible to please. For the last three weekends he had dragged her all over the city to look at houses he had no intention of buying. Emma's logical approach, armed with a checklist, had been summarily rejected on that first Saturday. 'A home should *feel* right,' Frazer had told her, confiscating her notebook. 'That's the sole criterion as far as I'm concerned; any-thing else can be fixed.' So how was it that every time they found a house that *felt* right there was some hideous engineering flaw that turned it into an untenable prop-osition? She firmed her lips. It was about time she put an end to all this shilly-shallying.

Frazer was quick to interpret the aggressive downturn or her luscious mouth. He spun on his heel and strode out of the room. 'Let's go back downstairs, there are one or two things I want to see again.'

'I don't know why we have to bother. You've already decided against it,' sniped Emma, and she followed him down the curving staircase. Frazer was dressed with the same casual splendour he had been when she'd first met him—pastel suit and silk shirt, topped off with sun-glasses that made it difficult to tell what he was thinking. She had stuck to her guns, refusing to admit this was anything more than an extension of her job, and had dressed accordingly: a cream linen skirt and navy blouse, its short sleeves being her only concession to casualness. She had even worn tights, though that decision she was beginning to regret. Even surrounded by the tempor-ising influence of the sea, Auckland was prone to scorching Februarys.

She trailed Frazer into the big, empty lounge. Out of the picture windows she could see Tom running around the big garden.

'Tom likes it,' she said, hopefully.

'It hasn't got a pool.'

'You're an engineer—build one! For goodness' sake, Frazer, it's a nice house, they've all been nice houses—why can't you make up your mind? You're not this indecisive in the office.' In fact he was already famous for his decision-making speed.

Frazer stopped his idle poking. 'So you like it. This is the kind of house you'd like to live in?'

'Well, not personally, no,' she said honestly, 'but I think it suits *you*...' She saw her mistake in the slight stiffening of his shoulders and had no doubt that behind the glasses his eyes were narrowing. 'I mean, it's the kind of house that anyone would feel comfortable in——'

'Anyone except you.'

'I...I just happen to prefer older houses. Houses with a bit of character.'

'And I don't? You see me in something soullessly modern?'

Was that how he saw this place? The same way she did?

'I...no...but you said a new house was what you wanted——'

'Maybe I was wrong.'

His cool about-face took her breath away. 'But you *told* the real-estate agency to put mostly new houses on the list——'

'I'm big enough to admit it when I make a mistake——'

Emma exploded. 'You mean we've wasted all this time for nothing!'

'I wouldn't exactly say for nothing, Emma. And don't forget that this house wasn't actually on the list.' They had been driving from one rejected house to the next when Frazer had seen the 'Open House' sign and insisted on stopping. 'At least I now know what I *don't* want and Tom's enjoyed the outings—in fact we've both enjoyed your company, even if you are a bit snappish at times——'

'Do you blame me? This was not supposed to be fun and games, you're supposed to be choosing a house!'

'And who said choosing a house couldn't be fun? Loosen up, honey, it's not the end of the world if we have to look at a few more.'

Emma had her own opinion about that, and she was about to icily inform him of it when the estate agent who had tactfully left them alone to wander the house came back into the room.

'Well, Mr Conway, what do you think?' The woman was fifty-five if she was a day but she had the girlish simper down to a fine art.

'Delightful, Ms Foulkes, but not *quite* what we had in mind.'

'Oh?' The coy smile hardly faltered. 'Anything specific?'

Emma had had enough. 'The soundproofing isn't adequate. Mr Conway is afraid that his antics in the bedroom might frighten the neighbours.'

The woman looked startled. Frazer coughed.

'Well, Mrs Conway, I think you'll find that when a house is fitted with carpets, drapes and furniture the sound-absorbing qualities of the furnishings will...er...make the rooms less...echoing,' the woman murmured.

Mrs Conway? Emma's mouth firmed. She was getting fed up with people assuming that she was in some way an appendage of Frazer's. 'We're not——'

'Now, honey, let's not embarrass Ms Foulkes with any more exciting revelations about our intimate life.' Frazer smoothly cut her off by the simple expediency of moving up behind her and pressing himself against her back, sliding an affectionate hand around her throat, his fingers stroking the madly beating pulse above her collarbone as his breath feathered the tiny strands of hair at the nape of her neck. 'Emma tends to have a rather...uninhibited attitude to certain things,' he confessed throatily.

It was exactly what she'd been thinking about him earlier and Emma went scarlet at the memory. Poor Ms Foulkes blushed in sympathy.

'I...I do have another couple in the kitchen...I'll just see if they want to look upstairs,' she muttered, and deserted them with unprofessional speed.

Emma knew she ought to move calmly out of his lightly restraining arms but she lingered, guiltily. She felt the soft abrasion of his teeth where the collar of her blouse had slipped sideways on her shoulder, and then the fiery stroke of his tongue, and came abruptly to her senses.

'What on earth made her think that we were married?' she demanded feverishly, pulling away.

'I have no idea.' Frazer let her go with a hint of lazy satisfaction as he watched her twitch nervously at her blouse. 'Perhaps the way you nag me.'

'I don't nag,' she said frostily.

'Contradict me, then. Or maybe it's those lascivious looks you keep sending my way.'

Her look was anything but lascivious. She pushed open the window and called out into the garden:

'Tom, time to go!'

'We haven't seen the wine cellar yet.'

Emma looked at him in exasperation. 'You look at the wine cellar. Tom and I will go and sit in the car.'

He shrugged. 'I don't have a wine collection anyway.'

With Tom skipping ahead of them they quickly extricated themselves from the slightly aggrieved Ms Foulkes and made their way back down the long, curving driveway. When they reached the car, Emma glared at it.

'Come on, Emma, it's only a car,' murmured Frazer as he helped Tom squeeze into the tiny compartment that passed as a rear seat.

'Girlie magazines have another word for it,' said Emma drily.

'Never read the things,' said Frazer virtuously.

'What word?' asked Tom, never one to be left out of the conversation for long.

Frazer smirked.

'Never you mind,' muttered Emma as she slid into the ridiculously low bucket seat of the fire-engine-red Ferrari.

'It's a phrase that means this car is a symbol of my masculinity,' said Frazer breezily, taking an unnecessary amount of care tucking Emma's skirt under her thigh, out of the way of the car door.

'How?' asked Tom, scrupulously clipping on the harness that Frazer had had fitted for him.

'It's long, smooth, sleek and incredibly exciting to women.'

'Frazer!' Emma's cool exterior was in danger of totally disintegrating, knowing that those wickedly provocative words were aimed at her, not his son. 'That's no way to talk in front of a child.'

'What did I say?' he asked, with an injured air.

Emma gave him the straight-mouthed look of menace that those associated with her knew was the equivalent of a hurricane warning. Only Frazer was foolish enough to tease her temper instead of soothing it. He seemed to *like* it when her frustration got the better of her. He laughed and started the engine, giving it a few extra revs of the throaty engine as he drew out into traffic, sending her a wicked glance as he did so. To her annoyance Emma thought that the sexy growl suited Frazer exactly.

'This really isn't a suitable car for transporting passengers, especially children,' she said dampeningly.

'What would you have me buy, a station-wagon?'

'Why not? It would certainly be more versatile than this macho banner.'

'But a lot less fun.' They stopped at a set of lights. A silver BMW pulled up beside them. The young man behind the wheel boasted all the hallmarks of a yuppie: young, good-looking, one elegant elbow laconically resting out his open window, a car phone glued to his ear. He finished his call and gave the Ferrari a slow survey, redolent of repressed envy. He looked up and caught Emma watching him. His eyes wandered over her in much the same way he had looked at the car. He smiled at her, picked up his phone receiver and raised his eyebrows questioningly. Conscious of Frazer beside her, observing her discomfort with patronising amusement, Emma felt annoyed enough with both men to take action. She fished in her bag and then wound down her window and extended a small, embossed card. The yuppie laughed, shooting a brief, challenging glance at Frazer as he plucked the card from her hand. He kissed it before he tucked it in his inside jacket pocket and Emma fluttered her eyelashes at him.

Frazer burned rubber pulling away from the lights, leaving the BMW idling in his dust.

'That was a business card, wasn't it? What in the hell did you do that for?' he smouldered, not longer patronising. 'That guy could be a maniac for all you know!'

For once Emma felt thoroughly in control. 'You're right, a Ferrari is fun,' she said cheerfully. 'Maybe I'll update my Honda to something less…conservative. How do you think I'd look in a Porsche? A jet-black Porsche with white leather seats?'

'Ridiculous!'

'I've got a Porsche. A toy one. It's white,' said Tom eagerly. 'Would you take me for a drive in yours, Emma?'

'Sure, kid. We can cruise the streets together.'

'Not with my son you don't!' Frazer exploded, almost grinding his precious gears. 'I can't believe you did something that irresponsible!' Emma could hardly believe it herself, but she wasn't sorry. It was nice to know she was capable of shocking him. That she wasn't entirely predictable! 'What are you going to do if he calls you?'

'He won't,' said Emma confidently.

'How do you know? You gave him the green light. You practically fell into his lap when you leaned out the window! Do you have your address on those things? He could turn up on your doorstep.' Her smile burned him into adding snidely, 'It's the car that really turned him on, you know, Emma, not you. It was envy, not lust. He couldn't take my Ferrari off me so he settled for trying to take the next best thing, my woman.'

Emma began to laugh. He had never heard her laugh so spontaneously and it should have pleased him that he had penetrated her reserve. Instead he was disgruntled, knowing that his behaviour was leaving him wide open to derision, but unable to shrug off his annoyance that she could flirt with a total stranger and yet turn the screws on him when he so much as looked at her. Her laughter was so infectious that Tom joined in. Now even his son found him funny!

'Goodness, if I'd realised that good-looking boy was such a bundle of pathological resentments I never would have fixed you up with him,' Emma said with mock horror.

'Huh?' The fact that she dismissed the lecher as a *boy* only slightly mollified him.

'It was one of *your* cards I gave him, Frazer, not mine.'

The car swerved slightly. 'Why, you devious little——'

'Next right,' she cut primly across his half-admiring fury, consulting the computerised list on her lap. 'The next house is just down here—there! Frazer! You missed the turn! I said right. Frazer, where are we going?'

'Lunch. Hungry, Tom?'

Emma knew it was useless to protest that they only had two more houses to look at, both near by. She had learned that she was no match for two hungry males. The first Saturday lunch had been at the Auckland Zoo. No one, as Emma knew from her experiences with her nephews and nieces, could remain aloof from baby hippos and newly-born orang-utans, and her resolution to keep everything brisk and businesslike very rapidly degenerated into a childish enthusiasm as Tom dragged her back and forth, trailed by his smug papa. The second weekend Emma had made it clear that she wasn't going to be hijacked out of the small property radius they were exploring and Frazer had agreed with a meekness she should have mistrusted—and taken them to the café at Kelly Tarlton's Underwater World on the waterfront. Naturally that had necessitated a trip below street-level to the renowned aquarium, and the invariably spooky sensation of being surrounded by tons of water, sharks and sting-rays and other denizens of the deep gliding silently overhead as they stood on the moving walkway in the glass viewing tunnel had quite taken Emma's mind off the fact that she was annoyed at Frazer.

'I told you that if you want to play tourist today you have to wait until you've dropped me off,' she now re-iterated the warning she had given him when he had collected her that morning. 'I've arranged to go out shopping with a friend later this afternoon.'

'Fine,' agreed Frazer equably. 'We'll look at the rest of the houses another day, but you can't go shopping without something inside you.' As usual with Frazer, her clear, precise directives were neatly overturned by a flurry of sweet, unarguable, and just plain wilful reason.

He turned into the stone gates of Cornwall Park and drove slowly down the tree-lined avenue, past the lunchtime joggers and cyclists, winding around One Tree Hill to where the observatory and children's playground were located.

'A picnic,' he confirmed her growing suspicion as he parked the car under a lacy pin-oak and turned to face her challengingly. 'It was Tom's idea. He wanted to go to the beach but I thought the park would be cooler, more tranquil...'

As if any woman could feel cool and tranquil with Frazer Conway looking at her like that! Emma busied herself helping Tom get his ball and other toys out of the boot, while Frazer carried the large hamper over to a tree which was a discreet distance from the other parents, mainly mothers, and toddlers taking advantage of the park. Tom ran off to climb a slide which wound around a tree trunk and Emma was about to follow when Frazer threw back the lid of the hamper and handed her a folded white cloth.

'Spread that out, will you, honey?'

She did so quickly. 'I think I'd better go and watch Tom.'

'He'll be all right, as long as he's within sight. Don't fret, Emma. Sit down and relax. You've earned your rest.' He thrust a glass of chilled white wine at her and she tucked her legs reluctantly under her as she watched him pull out plates and cutlery and container after container of food.

'Did you bring this from home, or buy it all?'

He sat back on his heels. 'Which would please you more?'

'Does it matter?'

'Pleasing you? Definitely. Have a peach.' He held it out to her and she imagined biting into the warm, juicy flesh and getting delectably messy and shook her head. She had to keep her dignity intact around Frazer...she was beginning to lose everything else!

'I'll peel and cut it up for you,' he said, and did so, handing the pieces to her on a plate of delicate white porcelain. He ate and fed her titbit by titbit, refusing to allow her to look into the containers and make her own choice from the gourmet selection. And everything that she ate, Frazer chose too, matching her bite for bite, swallow for swallow of wine. She couldn't very well object to his hunger, but somehow he had turned a simple matter of consumption into an oral seduction, an intimate sharing and mingling of tastes. Even Tom, running back every now and then to fetch something to maintain his energy, didn't disturb the subtle blend of rising tension.

'He has an awful lot of energy, doesn't he?' Emma murmured, shifting so that she was no longer facing directly into Frazer's lazy gaze. He had taken off his jacket and rolled up the sleeves of his shirt and lain back on the grass. He had tossed aside his sunglasses, too, since their heads were in the shade of the tree, and his eyes made her aware of every breath she took.

'A ton. Sally was like that, a bundle of fun.'

For some reason it made Emma uncomfortable whenever he mentioned his wife, and he seemed to do it quite often, as if he was thrusting the fact that he had been married relentlessly under her nose. Emma didn't want to be curious about Sally Conway, but Frazer made that impossible.

'You must have loved her very much.'

'Mmm. Of course I only married her for her dowry...'

'What?' More tendrils of hair escaped from Emma's sleek knot as she whipped her head back to him in shock.

He smiled, lying on his side, leaning his chin on his hand, his jacket carelessly discarded on the grass, the pale silk shirt pulling across his shoulders, parting another button over his deep chest, 'Sally was Andrew Freeman's—my business partner's—sister. Sally put some of her money into the business when we were

starting up, and worked for us as a secretary/recep-
tionist until we could afford to hire someone else. I guess
propinquity had something to do with our falling in love.
That and the fact that Sally was easy to love. Not beautiful but very warm and affectionate. She was blonde, too,
and small...' His musing eyes measured his memories
against Emma and she felt a sudden sickness. Was
Frazer's interest in her because she was like his late wife?

'After you hired another secretary, did—did your wife
keep on working for you?'

He shook his head. 'Sally was a home-maker at heart.
She helped out occasionally, and if we'd needed the
money after we got married she would have been happy
to get a job, but her professed vocation was "married
woman".' His reminiscent approval struck another dis-
sonant chord. A home-maker...every man's dream
woman! 'She was over the moon when she found she
was pregnant. She wanted kids by the dozen. I, on the
other hand, was more selfish. I didn't want to spread
her attentions too thinly. Sally was so unselfish and
overflowing with love that it was a constant battle to
protect her from her own impulsive heart. Tom is going
to be like that, I think—indulgently, even dangerously
generous to those he loves.'

'She sounds as if she was the perfect wife and mother,'
said Emma, looking down into her glass, seeing reflected there her own determination not to make that her
own epitaph.

'Oh, no, not perfect. We had our rows. Sally had a
hell of a temper. She might have looked and sounded
soft as marshmallow but when she got riled up about
one of her causes there were plenty of sparks. She may
not have had a career as you perceive it, but she was far
from a doormat——'

'I wasn't suggesting that she was,' said Emma.

'But the thought crossed your mind,' he said drily.
'You of all people, should be aware of the danger of

sticking labels on people. Human beings are too complex to be sorted into simple classifications, not least because they're constantly learning and growing and changing. I'm sure there are things you could teach me, Emma, about myself, and I'm damned sure there are a few things you need to learn from me...'

'Such as?'

'Trust.'

Emma gave him a sharp look. 'Trust? How can I trust you when I don't know you?'

'You know me better than you did three weeks ago. But I agree, you can't trust me until you trust yourself. You seem to be afraid that you're going to be coerced into something against your will——'

'Going to be? I already have been!' cried Emma.

'That was persuasion, not coercion; as a lawyer you should be aware of the difference.'

She was, and the infuriating part of it was that he was right. She was here because she had chosen to be, however reluctantly. She wasn't going down without a fight, however. 'You have some pretty suspect methods of persuasion. Some people might call it harassment!'

'In what way?' Trust him to want her embarrassment spelt out!

'Kissing me in the office——'

'And I enjoyed it,' he confessed serenely. 'So did you, Emma, which is, I suspect, what rankles so much. I let loose some human emotions in your buttoned-down sanctuary. But that was weeks ago and I've kept my lips to myself ever since. You must admit that I've been very circumspect around ConCorp lately. Maybe that's what's *really* upsetting you——'

'You...kissed me back there at the house——' she insisted wildly.

'That wasn't a kiss, that was a nibble. You want me to show you the difference?' He didn't move, but she felt the threat like a caress and spilled some of her wine on the white cloth.

'No! And that's another form of harassment. The things you say——'

'What kind of things?'

'You know very well!' she huffed.

'You mean because I act like a real live man and expect you to react accordingly? Come on, Emma, you enjoy arguing with me, goading me, annoying me. It puts a sparkle in those wonderful eyes——'

'The point is, I shouldn't have to—to——'

'Act like a woman?'

'Stop putting words in my mouth. And stop equating my sexuality with my identity as a woman——' She stopped. What on earth was that supposed to mean? She sounded like a naïve schoolgirl. 'I mean——'

'I know exactly what you mean, Emma. You're afraid of sex—not *per se*, but because it involves an emotional commitment to your womanhood that you're not prepared to make.'

'You don't know what you're talking about.'

'So? Explain it to me. Tell me what being a woman means to Emma Rainer.'

'I don't have to put up with this——'

'I thought you'd leap at the chance of straightening out my male-chauvinistic attitude. I'm asking you to talk, not to go to bed with me. Stop acting like a frightened virgin——' He hesitated as if a thought had just struck him with stunning force. 'You aren't, are you?' he asked cautiously.

'At my age?' she crackled. Did he think she was *that* 'buttoned-down' and behind the times? 'No!'

'Are you suffering from a sexual dysfunction——?'

'No!' Though it wouldn't be surprising, following the disaster with Phillip.

'Social disease?'

'How dare you?' She was becoming more wound up by the moment, while he was relaxing further into the short, sweet grass, lolling in front of her, a lazy, sunwarmed male basking in her vibrantly furious attention.

'But you're not very experienced——'

'What makes you say that?' she demanded, biting hard.

His eyes gleamed with amusement. 'Oh, little things...like how surprised you are when we both go up in flames at the lightest touch. Truth to tell, it took me by surprise at first, too, but there's a reserve about you that tells me that you haven't quite shaken off your small-town morals.'

'Nor do I want to,' she bristled. 'There's nothing wrong with choosing to be celibate. It's my right!'

'I completely agree,' he said delicately, although he had a strong impulse to get up and dance a jig at her inadvertent admission. 'Does that mean you're holding out for marriage?'

Her fleeting expression of horror stopped him in his tracks. Slowly he retraced his steps.

'It's the fear of marriage, not sex, isn't it, that makes you determined not to get involved?' he murmured, gingerly feeling his way through a minefield of possibilities. Of all the explanations for her hostility, this was the one he had least countenanced. In spite of her superficial chill, he sensed that Emma was far more a woman than many of the more blatantly feminine creatures who had flirted across his path.

'That's why finding out about Sally and Tommy has made you even more wary of your feelings for me,' he guessed shrewdly. 'Because it elevated me from the merely contemptible rake you first pegged me as, into the infinitely more dangerous category of Domesticated Male. Dangerous, that is, to a woman allergic to apron strings.' He laughed softly and without humour. 'And I thought it would show you that I was safe, trustworthy, honourable, and respectable! You're even more screwed up than I thought——'

'Because I don't want to get married at the drop of a hat?'

'No, because I think you've decided that marriage is out of the question entirely and for that reason you treat all men like potential enemies,' he said with the gentleness that was so shaming to her pride. 'Are your parents divorced?'

An equally horrifying thought. 'Of course not. They have a very happy marriage. So do my brothers and sisters.'

'Are you?'

'Am I what?'

'Divorced?' The hard consonants snapped the word together.

'I've never been married,' she said proudly.

'Not even a quick, here-today-gone-tomorrow teenage mistake?'

'No!'

'No one ever interested?'

'Too many,' blurted Emma truthfully, and then blushed. That sounded oh, so arrogant.

'Do tell,' he drawled, fascinated, rolling on to his stomach and propping his chin in his overlapped hands, his eyes reflecting the cloudless sky as he studied her flushed face.

'There's nothing to tell. It's just that, where I come from, people just assumed that my destiny, not to mention my duty, was to get married. Mothers pushed their sons at me because I was "approved". I would make a splendid farmer's wife.' Seduced by his patient silence, she went on to sketch out a scarcely recognisable picture of herself as a sweet, obedient daughter, a relentlessly kind-hearted little girl. A militant glint entered her eye. 'I remember that when I mentioned studying law to my careers adviser she laughed in my face. She didn't think I was cut out for law.'

'But you went for it anyway?'

'I had a brain, I wanted to use it. I resented being treated as if any career I chose would just be a stopgap until I settled down.'

'What about your family?'

'Oh, they were horrified, too. I was tough enough to be a farmer's wife but too soft to survive on my own out in the big wide world. My first few months away at university I was homesick but I didn't dare go back for weekends in case I never got away again.' She pulled a face. 'I wasn't half as confident as I pretended to be, but I was determined. There *were* times when I wanted to throw in the towel and run away from the pressures, the necessity not only to succeed but to do better than anyone else so that no one would be able to attach a rider to my success...I *had* to get Honours. It was a matter of principle.'

'I see.' And he did, all too clearly. 'And you succeeded. That must have silenced your critics.'

Emma laughed ruefully. 'Don't you believe it. They're still waiting for me to fall on my face so they can say "I told you so".'

'Do you really believe that your family and friends are that disloyal?'

Emma stiffened at the note of criticism, then forced herself to admit honestly, 'No, not really. At least, they don't see it as disloyalty. They just want me to be happy—*their* way.'

'But they must be proud of your achievements——'

'Oh, they do their share of boasting around town, I suppose but...' She laughed, this time wistfully. 'I just have this feeling that I've disappointed them in some way. I don't know...I can't explain it.'

'And yourself? Have you disappointed yourself?'

She reared up. 'Of course not! I've done everything I wanted to do, and done it damned well; *better* than well. I'm damned proud of what I am, and what I do.'

'Then that's all that matters. As long as you respect yourself, you can command the respect of others. Maybe you're the one who still sees yourself the way your family used to see you. Maybe you're the one putting up the barriers to understanding. You can be very prickly and defensive where your career is concerned, I suppose as a matter of past necessity. Isn't it time that you accepted the reality of your success? No one can take away your past accomplishments, Emma. Ambition is laudable, but if you let it take too fierce a hold on you you'll spend your whole life striving for what's just out of reach, never being satisfied with what you've got. That can make a person very bitter... very lonely.'

Her lovely mouth twisted sardonically. 'Funny, that's what Phillip said——' Damn! How did he make her, a lawyer, so loose with her confidence?

'Who's Phillip?' He was there, on the instant, prying.

'No one you'd know,' she said stonily, summoning sarcasm to her rescue. 'And how exactly do you think I ought to accept "the reality of my success"?'

He let it go... for the moment. 'Loosen up. Relax. Smell the roses. Stop thinking that every man, woman and child is only lying in wait to ambush you on the route to glorious self-determination. Round out your personality. Have a tumultuous affair!'

'With you?' she asked disdainfully.

'Well, certainly not with the jerk in the BMW! Yes, with me. Why don't we let some sunlight in on this dark attraction between us? Who knows, it might prove to be a shadowy illusion after all? You might find that the only thing you have to fear is fear itself...'

So... he wanted an affair that would cure them both of an unwelcome physical infatuation. Emma scrambled to her knees, crumpled and hot and sticky, furious at how gullible she had almost been as she shovelled the picnic things back in the hamper. She had briefly experienced the devastating feeling that Frazer had understood... To be understood—ah, how seductive that prospect was. She had trembled on the edge of discovery; she had *wanted* to fall. She had actually been studying his mouth as it shaped his words, wondering what it would be like to lie down with him in the sweet grass and feel it move over her sun-silked skin, shaping her desire to his needs...

She might have known that it was *his* needs that were foremost in his mind. Emma might have made it clear that she wasn't interested in strings, but he didn't have to act so pleased about it!

And as for intimating that sleeping with him was the simple solution to all her problems...

Frazer wasn't the solution; he was the problem!

CHAPTER SEVEN

'GORGEOUS, isn't she?'

The sibilance was a serpent's hiss in Emma's ear.

'Who?' Emma feigned puzzlement but Edward's smile as he slithered up beside her was knowing.

'The cute little redhead draped over our lord and master.'

Emma's eyes skimmed the crowd of ConCorp personnel, as if she hadn't been staring hard at the couple a few moments before. 'Yes, she's very pretty.'

'You know who she is, of course...'

Emma shrugged. 'Stuart and I have only just arrived. I haven't had a chance to circulate yet.'

She knew that would stun him into a diversion from his gloating and she was right. 'Stuart? You mean *Grayson*? You came with Stuart Grayson!'

Emma smiled serenely at his chagrin. Naturally he had assumed that once Stuart had 'scooped the pool', so to speak, he would have dropped Emma like a hot coal. Emma had assumed as much herself, but Stuart had proved to be a nicer man than either of them had given him credit for. Not only had he confessed up-front about the bet, but he had asked for a second date before the first was over. Emma had liked him in spite of herself. He made her laugh...and he didn't try to tie her up in physical and mental knots. She hadn't been able to resist the temptation to invite him along to the ConCorp end-of-the-financial-year party. Usually it was held at a hotel but this year Sir Clive was hosting it at his private home. Emma wondered whether this departure from tradition was fresh evidence of the more relaxed style of business that Frazer was promoting at ConCorp. He was certainly looking pretty relaxed tonight...

'He *claims* that she's his son's live-in American nanny, but they look a bit too cosy to be strictly employer and employee, wouldn't you say? And you're an expert on cosiness these days... I mean, what kind of man escorts his son's *nanny* to a business function?'

Emma's icy composure slipped. 'That's Jennifer?' she murmured numbly. Tom had told her that 'Jen' would be coming to New Zealand after she had had a holiday. He had chattered about how nice she was, and how clever, and how she knew lots of games, and how she had been the one to look after him whenever his daddy went away. Emma had imagined a pleasant, cheerful, motherly lady of uncertain years.

'Poor Emma,' Edward commiserated slyly. 'Didn't you know about Lolita? All the time you've been trying to ingratiate yourself with Conway, he's had *that* tucked away at home, waiting for him...'

'Try and control your drooling, Edward,' said Emma coldly. 'I doubt that even Frazer would be as brave as to flaunt a liaison in Sir Clive and Lady Dorothy's faces, knowing how they feel about that sort of thing...' She wondered why she was bothering to try and defend him. His arm was around the redhead's waist now, and he was looking down at her with the tenderly teasing expression that Emma had seen him use with Tom. It was both possessive and loving. Oh, *God*...

'No wonder he was so anxious for you to find him a house. He wants to re-establish his little love-nest. And you're helping him, Emma. I never knew you were such a romantic!'

'Oh, shut up, Edward! Why don't you keep your smutty speculation to yourself?'

'Speculation, hell! Look at her, Emma. Look at her and tell me that any red-blooded man could live day in day out with all that female pulchritude and not succumb to his hormones!'

And Frazer was certainly red-blooded. Emma felt an unpleasant and unfamiliar sensation of heat churning in her stomach. Not heat—jealousy; pure, boiling jealousy. And self-contempt that she had almost believed that Frazer was, in his own weird and aggravating way, courting her. After the abrupt end to their picnic the previous weekend he had sent her flowers every day. No messages, just the flowers, fresh, beautiful, each perfect stem an exquisite reproach. And he had sent them not only to her home but to her office, too, prompting a rash of speculation among her colleagues as to the identity of the sender. And to think she had actually been weakening...

Edward, having delivered his poisonous thrust, happily withdrew to spread his scurrilous rumours elsewhere, probably with extra embellishment about her and Stuart, but she didn't even notice him leave; she was too busy trying to ignore the impulse to smash things.

'Was that Edward? I would have liked to say hello.' It was Stuart, bearing two glasses of champagne, the twinkle in his soft brown eyes telling her that he would have enjoyed seeing the other man disconcerted by his presence. Stuart had a very well-developed sense of humour. In that respect he was a bit like Frazer...

'Mmm, just what I need to wash the taste away,' said Emma wryly, taking the proffered drink when she felt more like asking for a good slug of mind-numbing whisky. She sipped, and gradually forced herself to relax by concentrating ruthlessly on Stuart's light, amusing patter.

So intent was she on blocking everything else out that she was taken off guard by a silky murmur from behind. 'You seem to be enjoying yourself rather more freely than usual tonight, Emma. If *you* let your hair down, then the party *must* be a raging success!' Frazer flipped a casual finger through the smooth, shiny, ice-blonde bob that flared around her shoulders as she flinched haughtily away. His hand fell. He held her defiant gaze for a moment before nodding coolly at her companion. 'Grayson. Good to see our legal colleagues represented here tonight.'

Emma didn't give her companion time to reply. 'I'm sorry if we're late but we went out to dinner first,' she took great pleasure in telling him.

Frazer transferred his steely blue stare from her bland companion back to herself. 'Did you, indeed? I hope you had a pleasant meal?' He made it sound as if it might be the last one she ever ate. A little arc of tension sparked between them.

'Pleasant is a little...pallid...to describe the experience of dining with Emma,' interceded Stuart smoothly. 'Enchanting might be nearer the mark. Emma is always a stimulating companion.'

Always? Emma saw Frazer digest the implications of that remark, and hurriedly gulped some more of her champagne. Perhaps it hadn't been such a good idea, after all, to flaunt Stuart under his nose. Then her eye fell on a red beacon across the room. Another gulp or two and her spine stiffened again. Champagne was certainly a great source of foolish bravado.

'Then, since you've already had such a...stimulating evening so far you won't mind if I borrow Emma for a dance,' said Frazer equally smoothly, cupping her elbow with a sure touch that sent bubbles tilting wildly in her glass.

'Actually I do——' began Stuart mildly, taking her other elbow, a glimmer of amusement betraying his realisation that he was a bit-player in a wider game. Frazer recognised the glimmer and the men exchanged a long, measuring look of masculine communications that infuriated Emma.

'It's got nothing to do with Stuart. Why don't you ask me if *I* mind?' demanded Emma aggressively. 'It's my decision what I do and where I go and with whom.'

Frazer grinned. 'Shall we toss for her?'

To Emma's fury Stuart actually grinned back. 'No, thanks. I think the lady is quite capable of tossing both of us right back.'

'Woman, Grayson, not lady. Emma doesn't like to be labelled a lady, do you, honey?' Before she had time to frame a vitriolic reply he said meekly, 'All I wanted to do was introduce you to Jenny. She's dying to meet you.'

Emma required all her legal training to keep a poker face, while inside she was all spitting fury.

'Is Jenny the redhead? I wouldn't mind meeting her myself,' murmured Stuart appreciatively.

Frazer's expression was wiped clear of amusement. 'She's too young for you, Grayson.'

'But not for you, obviously,' said Emma sarcastically.

Frazer didn't even look at her. 'She's under my protection,' he told Stuart softly. 'Any man who lays a hand on her answers to me. Stick to more experienced game and leave me and mine alone.'

Emma had had no reason to trust Edward. She knew he enjoyed causing trouble, liked watching her squirm. She hadn't wanted to believe him, but now, here was Frazer claiming the girl publicly as his. Warning other men off. She hadn't liked the helpless sensation of being fought over by the two men. She discovered she liked even less their crossing swords over another woman.

Stuart gave in gracefully, inclining his head. 'In that case you'll have no objection to my keeping Emma. I rather think she's a full-bodied claret to your frothy rosé. Emma, shall we dance?'

Much as her feminist principles were offended by that mocking little metaphor, Emma felt a burst of malicious pleasure as Frazer smouldered at the pointed thrust.

'Delighted, Stuart.' With a little twist Emma pulled her elbow out of Frazer's grasp, handed him her empty glass and floated into Stuart's arms. As he whipped her on to the glossy dance-floor, she smiled brilliantly over his shoulder into a brooding blue stare and said sweetly, 'Run along, Frazer, before some other wolf with a fixation for youth gobbles up your Little Red Riding Hood.'

She was breathless as Stuart waltzed her away. For a moment she had thought Frazer was going to make a scene. Her vitriolic taunt had provoked a brilliant sunflare of emotion in the cerulean eyes, a hot and reckless surge of triumph that had been both terrifying and exciting.

'Is there a knife in my back?' murmured Stuart as he turned her, and caught sight of Frazer, pacing them at the edge of the floor.

'Mmm?' Emma elected to play innocent.

Stuart tilted his head back so he could see her lightly flushed face. 'You can't kid a kidder, Emma. I like you but I have a highly refined sense of self-preservation. I'm afraid you're going to have to leave me out of your private battles from now on.' His smile was wry and flatteringly regretful. 'Besides, methinks in this case the lady prefers the dragon to the knight anyway...'

'Ah, but as Frazer pointed out, I'm not a lady,' said Emma crisply, not wanting to give anything away.

Stuart laughed. 'Maybe I have my characters mixed up. Maybe *you're* the dragon. You were certainly breathing fire back there!'

She was breathing fire later, too, when Frazer cut abruptly in on a close conversation she was having with Sir Clive and Lady Dorothy, both of whom seemed rather unfairly amused by her failure to find Frazer's dream house. Sir Clive had the gall to pat her with one hand, and cuff her with the other, praising her for working 'so well in harness' with his half-brother but ordering her 'not to be so prickly' with the poor boy after hours. What on earth had the *poor boy* been telling them?

'I don't want to dance with you!' she hissed at Frazer as he steered her grimly on to the floor.

'Too bad.' As she stiffened in his arms he threatened softly. 'Follow my lead, Emma, or I swear I'll *drag* you around this floor. And smile. Smile as if your life depended on it. Because at this moment it quite probably does.' He spun her neatly, thrusting his thigh hard between hers as he reversed their direction and Emma gasped. 'Like that?' he asked her wolfishly. 'The real thing is even better.'

'You really are disgusting,' she said shakily, feeling oddly weak and wobbly as his leg withdrew.

'I'm blunt. And I don't like you using other men to annoy me.'

'I wasn't——'

'You were. You're not seriously interested in Grayson. How can you trust a man who dates you for a bet? How do you know he hasn't laid money on how soon he can get you into bed?'

Emma flushed angrily, knowing there was no way out but the truth, now that Stuart had summarily retired from the field. 'Because he knows I have no intention of going to bed with him.' She ignored Frazer's soft grunt of satisfaction. 'We understand each other perfectly well and we happen to enjoy each other's company.'

'And you needed someone to hide behind,' he guessed. 'Or did you intend to make me jealous?'

'Why should I want to make you jealous?' Emma spat at him.

'To test my sincerity, perhaps? Well, it worked. I was as jealous as hell. Like you...'

'Like me what?'

'Oh, Emma, honey... never try and play dumb, it doesn't suit you.' His amusement sent a shivery trickle down her spine as his body blocked hers, advancing, retreating, the dance steps becoming a teasing ritual, guiding her every move. 'Red Riding Hood, remember? Your razor tongue shredding an innocent young girl you don't even know? Jealousy has an unmistakable ring to it.'

'I don't imagine she stayed innocent very long around you!'

'Don't you?' He brushed his cheek against her hair. 'Why?'

It was bizarre, the counterpoint of bodily intimacy and verbal war. Bizarre and ... arousing. To her horror Emma felt a tingling in her breasts as they absorbed the heat from his body. Her dress was long and black, a strapless top offset by a broad brocade belt, the skirt full and swirly. The black lace bra she wore was little better than a quarter-cup and she was terrified that if she moved away the sharp crests of her nipples would be obvious against the tight, thin silk-jersey bodice.

'I only said what everyone else is thinking,' Emma defended herself distractedly.

'Not everyone, surely. Those people who have actually *welcomed* an introduction to my sister-in-law would find it ludicrous to suggest that a girl who for the past eight years has called me "uncle" and behaved like a fond daughter would harbour any sexual interest in me, or me in her.'

Emma only heard the first part of the second sentence. 'Y ... your sister-in-law?'

'Jenny Freeman.'

'B-but, she has red hair!' was all Emma could think to stammer.

'So has Andrew. Sally was the odd one out, a throwback to her Swedish great-grandmother.'

'But, she's so young——'

'Not quite as young as she looks. She's nineteen. Jenny was a late baby and Sally practically brought her up when their parents died. She moved in with us when we were married. She's a good kid but no academic, and there was no way I could stop her leaving school as soon as she legally could. Her best subject was domestic science so she decided that the perfect solution to the problem of her job and my difficulty in looking after Tom was that I should employ her as a full-time nanny-housekeeper. Up until now it's worked out perfectly. There was no one I'd rather have trusted than Jen. She may look like a beautiful butterfly but she's very down-to-earth. At seventeen she had more common sense in her little finger than a lot of natural mothers ever acquire.'

He seemed to be waiting for something. An apology, maybe. Emma averted her face and said stiffly, 'You deliberately let me think——!'

'Let?' He scorned her excuse. 'As if I had much choice in the matter. You work hard at thinking the worst of me.'

'Edward said——'

'Oh, I see...' It was a poor defence and they both knew it. 'Cleaver, whom you believe to be a raging male chauvinist who would tread on his own grandmother to get ahead, is suddenly an impeccable source.'

His sarcasm, so well-deserved, lacerated her pride. 'She was hanging all over you; what was I supposed to think?'

'You're a lawyer. You should have known better to make a judgement before all the evidence was in. But, of course, one must expect this kind of emotionalism from a woman. It's the very thing that's hampered the feminist movement all along, this regrettable tendency to take everything so *personally*...'

If it had been any other man Emma would have kicked him in the shins. But this was Frazer. She knew he didn't subscribe to the garbage he was spouting. She remained rigidly silent until he goaded, 'I suppose darling Phillip was of the same opinion——'

She arched abruptly back against his restraining arms. 'Who told you about Phillip?' she snapped. It *was* just the kind of thing Phillip had thrown at her in their last argument. But, as far as she knew, no one at ConCorp knew about her ex-fiancé...

'You did. On our picnic. Remember?' He smiled down into her suspicious face, no doubt supremely aware of how sexy that tilt of his mouth was.

'I didn't say anything about him.'

'I know, it was what you didn't say that intrigued me. Was he the one who scared you off marriage?'

'I told you. I just don't want to get married.'

'But did you want to marry Phillip?'

She tried to stop dancing but his strength supported them both easily, manipulating her like a puppet.

'We're going to dance until you tell me,' said Frazer, still smiling. But his eyes had gone a steely shade of grey-blue that indicated Frazer at his most stubborn, most determined. In such a mood, Emma had learned, he was not to be thwarted, and suddenly she didn't have the energy to try. What did it matter, anyway?

She began moving her feet again, albeit with dragging steps that signalled her displeasure.

'Phillip and I went through law school together. We were just friends for the first few years, always vying for the top position in class—which he usually got. He was very clever. We had lots of things in common. We liked the same things, we were both intending to specialise in corporate law, and both got offers from the same firm in our final year. It just seemed like...a perfect match.'

'You were in love with him?'

'He...I...he seemed so perfect for me.' She didn't notice the automatic evasion, but Frazer did. 'We got engaged halfway through our final year.'

'You keep mentioning the word perfect. That sounds ominous for a start,' murmured Frazer drily. 'Perfection is rarely what it first seems.'

'I couldn't believe the way he changed in the last few months. I mean, he knew how much the law meant to me, he knew how good I was. For heaven's sake, I beat him into second place in the Finals!'

'Aahhh.' It was a soft breath of revelation, but Emma was in full flight with her memories.

'All those years at university he quite happily encouraged my ambitions and yet suddenly, when we qualified and were working together, it turned out he wanted something entirely different. Suddenly it wasn't a partner he wanted, it was a *wife*...the kind of wife who stayed at home and helped boost her husband up the ladder of success. Oh, I could work for the first few years of our marriage, but after that he wanted me to stay home with the children...not just until they started school, but until they finished *high* school!' Her voice rose in an echo of her outrage. 'He said that children needed the stable constant of at least one parent at home. Fine, that was his opinion, but it never occurred to him that *he* take any time off from his career to be the constant parent—oh, no, that was strictly a female task. After all the discussions about equality that we'd had, he could turn around and say that! He was so...inflexible!'

'And were you just as inflexible?'

'Naturally I would have taken some maternity leave,' she said stiffly. 'But he wanted more than that. He wanted what I'd gone to university precisely to *escape*——'

'It sounds to me as if he found he couldn't take the competition, but didn't have the guts to admit it,' commented Frazer quietly.

'That's ridiculous!' Emma declared. 'One of the reasons we got on so well together was because we shared the same goals, because I was as intelligent and articulate as he was——'

'Not as, but *more*,' Frazer pointed out. 'He respected your aspirations, sure, but only as long as you weren't a threat to his. You not only got a better degree than he did, you were going to work alongside him, continually challenging his position and self-image. You're a very bright star, Emma...beauty, brains, dedication—it takes a very secure man to cope with that. If he had really loved you, he'd have tried to work it out. If not, he'd look for a way out that didn't damage his ego—try and make *you* somehow responsible for *his* weakness. I bet you not only let him off the hook personally but professionally, too. Is that when you came to work for ConCorp?'

'I—yes,' she stammered, stunned by his swift and devastatingly perceptive analysis. Looking back on it, she realised that Phillip *had* deliberately provoked her in that row that had broken up their engagement. He had always seemed so confident, even opinionated, but what if his self-confidence had been flawed, dependent on always feeling that he was top dog? All this time she had despised herself for not seeing him for what he was, but if Phillip had hidden his weakness even from himself she had nothing to castigate herself for. Suddenly she felt more light-headed than mere champagne alone could account for.

'His loss, our gain,' said Frazer laconically. 'I get the impression that the thrills in this abortive romance of yours were largely of the intellectual kind. Fine for colleagues, or even friends, but it leaves a lot to be desired in an affair, let alone a marriage...literally.'

Suddenly she noticed where he had led her unwary steps. They had danced out of the huge, formal lounge into a wide, carpeted corridor. 'What are we doing here?'

'I didn't think you wanted anyone speculating on the intimate nature of our conversation.'

'It wasn't very intimate——' Emma protested, trying to resist his inexorable flow.

'No, but it's going to be.' With a quick gesture he threw open a door to his left and twisted inside it, drawing her with him and snapping the door closed behind them.

'What are you doing?' she said furiously, as he fumbled for the light switch and flicked on the dim yellow light. 'This is a cupboard, for goodness' sake!'

'Linen closet,' he corrected as he let her go and leaned back against the door. 'And goodness has nothing to do with it. Any small, enclosed space with you suggests a number of sinful possibilities. Tell me you don't want me to kiss you, Emma...'

His saying it in that liquid honey drawl made instant compliance impossible. Emma wavered, suddenly remembering every other time that he had kissed her...touched her...and what it had felt like. His eyes were hot and dark, hot as his kisses, dark as the desires he roused. Her own mouth was dry and it was a struggle to breathe. The cupboard was quite large, lined with shelves packed with table linen which had a close, deadening effect. There was no sound in the little room except their ragged breathing. Emma was powerless to object when he reached out and trailed a finger across her shoulders.

'I like your dress.'

'It...' Her voice momentarily failed her. His featherlight touch was igniting little fires under her skin. She forgot about the party, the world outside the cupboard. 'It's new...'

'I don't often see you in a dress. You usually wear suits...your metaphorical armour. You're so pale...' The finger dipped and glided, tracing a pattern down to the upper swell of her breasts.

'I...I don't get out in the sun much. I...I'm too busy...'

'You have very delicate skin. You'd probably burn easily anyway,' he murmured, watching the progress of his finger. 'It's as smooth and rich as cream. It bet it's like that all over.' His eyes rose to hers, his finger sliding lightly into the cleft between her breasts. 'But it wouldn't taste the same all over... in some places it would be soft and sweet, and in others tart and fresh. Would you like me to taste you all over, Emma...?'

She was going to faint! Her head felt heavy and dizzily light at the same time. She was taking shallow, rapid breaths that lifted her breasts to his touch. She had never felt like this before...so devastated by a few evocative words.

'Frazer...' She knew there was some reason she should protest, but for the life of her, the love of her, she couldn't remember it.

'You don't have to pretend with me, Emma,' he told her huskily. 'I'm not afraid of you. I love it when you test yourself against me. With me you can always feel free to be yourself. Are you wearing anything under the dress?'

Her lips parted. Her eyes were dark, gold-rimmed discs in the soft yellow light. She nodded dumbly.

'Can I see...?'

He wanted her to take off her dress for him? Here? Emma quivered with the delicious shock of it. She had always thought of herself as cool and sophisticated, but Frazer was showing her how innocent she really was— innocent, and prudish...and secretly wicked. She wanted to take it off, wanted him to look at her body...want her...love her...

'I...can't...' she whispered, reaching for the tattered rags of her self-control. He smiled, and there was such a tender compassion in that smile that she trembled anew. His other hand came up, and he softly cupped her breasts, stilling their frantic movement.

'Let me ... Don't be afraid. Trust me, Emma. I'm not going to make love to you, not here. All I want is a small taste ... a promise of things to come ...'

She stared fixedly at his face as his fingers curled into the soft jersey and he slowly eased the top of her dress down, pushing it into folds around her narrow waist, holding it there. She watched, fascinated, the tanned, handsome face harden, his breath hissing through his teeth as he looked at what he had uncovered. A tinge of dark blood anointed his slanting cheekbones, his pupils expanding like black storm-clouds in the hot blue sky.

'Is this new, too?' he asked softly, no trace of honey in his voice now, only rough, jagged edges that snagged at her senses as he touched the lacy side of her daring bra.

'I ... yesss ...' If only he would touch her properly, instead of tormenting her with his tantalising eyes.

'Did you wear it for me?'

Her head fell back on her shoulders, baring the truth. 'Yes!' When she had bought the dress and wispy underwear she had told herself it was because she wanted to do the company proud. But she had lied, she knew that now. She had wanted to look sexy for Frazer. Not only to look sexy, but to feel sexy too. To taunt him with what she was denying him ... beckoning him on only to push him away. But she could no more deny him tonight than she could deny herself. Her attack of jealousy had unlocked something in her heart. She needed this, as much as he did ... more ...

'Then I guess I can ask you *not* to wear it for me, too ...' And yet he stilled her hand when she reached behind her for the clasp. 'But not yet ... not yet ... Oh, God ... I love the way you're made, the way you look, the way you move, the way you think ... I love everything about you, honeysweet ...'

He stroked her through the flimsy fabric, following the delicate interweaving of the pattern, round and round and round on the underside of her breasts until she was arching with agony, the ache so intense that it felt as if her swollen breasts were imprisoned in iron rather than the softest of French lace.

'Please...'

Frazer was generous in granting her request. His thumbnail skimmed the lace that rimmed the low-cut top of her bra and dipped, catching on the rigid nipple that peeped from its ruffled nest. Emma cried out and his mouth came down on hers, smothering her pleasure as his thumb scraped and scraped again, first the nail and then the lightly callused pad, stinging and soothing, drawing out the lace's captive until it brushed his pleated shirtfront. He shifted her to one side, his mouth still devouring hers, and turned his exquisite attention to freeing her other breast, teasing it with fingers that felt cool to the fiery heat blooming under her skin.

He lifted his mouth and groaned at the sight of her, naked to the waist, aflame with a passion that fuelled his, her wide mouth lush and full and moist for his pleasure, an erotic dream in itself. Then he was lifting her, pushing her back on to one of the wider lower shelves, moving in between her thighs, pressing hot and tight and close, whispering of forbidden delights as he urged her to feel what she did to him, no longer the slow, sensuous lover but all blind, driving masculinity taking everything he could get and wanting still more...

His mouth on her breasts was their undoing. Emma gave a small, whispery scream as he bit into the swollen ripeness to suckle with a strong, rhythmic, hungry impatience that wrenched at her womb. The sound was short and sharp and penetrating. It shocked them both out of their sensory haze.

With a low, hoarse groan Frazer straightened jerkily, forcing her to do the same as he pulled her violently against his own aching fullness before letting her slide slowly back down his body. Her feet touched the ground in more ways than one. They stared at each other, panting wildly, aware of what had just almost happened. Emma gave a broken cry and pressed her hands over her aroused breasts, flushing deeply at his expression of intensely male satisfaction.

She half expected him to gloat, but she wronged him yet again. 'I've marked you,' he muttered thickly.

She followed his gaze and saw the faint bruises appearing on the creamy plumpness exposed between her protectively splayed fingers. Evidence of his passion. Hers, too...

'I didn't hurt you, though, did I? You liked it when I was a little rough...'

She had. Too much. 'Oh, God, what have I done?' she muttered shakily, struggling to pull up her bra and the bodice of her dress, almost tearing them in her hurry.

'You acted spontaneously, Emma. We both did. Only the time and place were wrong, not what we did. Next time it'll be different... better... Here, let me.' He dealt with her problem deftly, without fuss. He had made his point, and now it was up to his cautious, impulsive Emma to come to terms with it in her own inimitable fashion. Tonight was a turning-point for both of them. After tonight she could not deny there were times in her life when the needs of the woman were paramount over the needs of the lawyer, the businesswoman, and that he was a man supremely capable of meeting those needs. And after tonight he would no longer protect her from the seriousness of his intentions, no longer pretend that he wasn't fathoms deep in love with her, and proud of it!

'Don't *do* that!' Emma hissed as Frazer finally moved to fling open the door on the real world again. 'Someone might see us come out!' She was avoiding his eyes, patting at her hair and pulling at a dress which suddenly seemed too tight for her.

'You look fine, Emma,' Frazer soothed, adding gently, 'A little . . . flushed and mellow, but then that's expected of you at a party.'

Emma sent a haughty look skimming past his ear. 'Let me go first. And tidy yourself up before you come out,' she ordered. Frazer merely grinned back at her, as if reminding her that *he* was the one who had pulled back, not her. How humiliating!

But it seemed she had not yet plumbed the depths of her humiliation. After carefully opening the door a crack to check the coast was clear, she took a deep breath and slipped out of the cupboard—just as Sir Clive, flanked by Edward and Jasper, emerged from the doorway opposite.

The three men looked at her automatically and, fatally, her guilt made her hesitate. As she did so the door behind her swung open again, catching her heel and nudging her out of the way, revealing the shelves of linen . . . and a rather sexily rumpled Frazer.

Now *that* was humiliation!

CHAPTER EIGHT

'I HOPE this house you found for the Conways has plenty of *closet* space in it.'

'Marc! If you make one more, just *one* more joke about closets...' Emma let her voice trail off menacingly.

'Sorry.' Her secretary grinned at her unrepentantly.

'Besides, I've heard them all before, *ad nauseam*,' said Emma grimly. 'I don't think there's anyone in the city who hasn't heard that wretched story.'

'Just be thankful it didn't make the papers. I wouldn't have put it past Edward to make an anonymous call to some sleazy rag...'

Emma shuddered. Edward probably would have done just that, if he didn't figure the damage already done to her reputation was sufficiently crippling to knock her out of contention.

She would never forgive Frazer for the brazen way he had strolled out of that closet and back into the party, leaving Emma behind to stammer explanations to the goggling trio. She would have done better to have followed Frazer's lead and just walked off with at least the shreds of her dignity. As it was, her gabble about checking out Frazer's storage requirements for his new house had only succeeded in damning her completely. Later Edward had cornered her in the supper-room, triumphant that all his darkest suspicions about her had finally been confirmed, and lashed her with an open contempt that went far beyond his usual insinuating sneers.

'Of course, you realise that no one in the company can possibly take you seriously any more...a bimbo who

134

has it off in cupboards at parties,' he finished with savage satisfaction. 'I never would have thought you'd go that far, Emma. Arrogant you may be, but you've never been reckless. Maybe seeing the redhead with her hooks into Conway made you panic. I hope you got what you wanted in there because you sure as hell aren't going to get it out here. If anyone had any doubts about your questionable methods of lobbying for promotion they're blowing in the wind now. You can kiss goodbye to any directorship while Clive still has a say in the company. Did you see his face? He practically had a heart attack— bit his cigar clean in half! You'll be damned lucky to keep any job at all with ConCorp, let alone any other position of responsibility in this city...'

She had taken everything he had thrown at her in white-faced silence. She hadn't attempted to make any excuses because there *were* none. She hadn't been using Frazer as a short cut to power but it was preferable that Edward think that than know the truth—that she had been temporarily insane. That Emma Rainer had lost her head over a man. Emma was more horrified than he at what had happened. She had done something that she had vowed she never would...she had compromised her professional and personal integrity in the name of love. Love, the grand delusion!

She had stayed on at the party only long enough to find Lady Dorothy and make a truthful excuse—a headache—for her early departure. She had taken a taxi home, quite forgetting about Stuart, who had been excruciatingly diplomatic when she had rung the next day to apologise. He hadn't asked any awkward questions, doubtless because he already knew the answers. Edward must have worked the room like lightning after she left. Certainly by the time she arrived at the office the next day the smirks had already been doing the rounds, and her next encounter with Frazer had added fuel to the wildfire rumours, for it had ended with a very public row.

She had dreaded a summons to his office all morning, had known that Frazer wouldn't let her escape the consequences of her passionate recklessness the night before, and had worked up a fine head of steam when the message didn't come until the afternoon.

As soon as she stepped inside his office she realised her temper was a mistake. She should have chilled down her emotions, not stoked them up. When Frazer tried to take her in his arms and apologise for the unavoidable delay she reacted explosively, shoving him away and spewing out accusations, including the wild suggestion that he had deliberately compromised her at the party in order to sabotage her promotion.

'Don't get me mixed up with that wimp Phillip, Emma,' Frazer growled, stirring to life. 'I told you you have nothing to fear from me——'

'Nothing to fear!' Emma repeated stormily. 'You've destroyed my professional reputation, rendered me a dirty joke to my colleagues and left my integrity wide open to question. What else *is* there to fear?'

'You're acting as if it were entirely my fault, Emma,' he said, prowling away from her and back again. 'It takes two to tango. So we got caught acting like lovers. So what? It may have been a little embarrassing, but I don't see why you should act as if we've committed an unspeakable crime. As far as I know there's no law in this, or any other country, forbidding working colleagues from personal involvement. Even if there was it would be unworkable. Love ignores rules and regulations... Love makes its own rules...'

Emma was disconcerted by the warmth of his words and the contrasting cool determination in the blue eyes. Love... Hadn't Frazer murmured that forbidden word last night, somewhere in the white-heat of the moment? And hadn't she wondered what it would be like to give more to this man than just her body? *Love*. The steel barrier around her heart shivered with the force of the acknowledged blow. Shivered but didn't give way. No, not love...not with Frazer. *Especially* not with Frazer. He was all wrong for her. He had Tom...he admired domesticated women like Sally and his sister-in-law...there were any number of reasons why she couldn't love him and he couldn't, shouldn't love her. Just saying it wasn't going to make it so. Panic clawed at her, reinforcing the barriers.

'So what are you saying? That we may as well sleep together because everyone already *thinks* we are? I'm ruined anyway so what's the difference?' Her voice was textured with shrill rejection.

'No, that's not what I'm saying. You're taking this too seriously. It'll be a nine-day wonder——'

'Nine days too long!' Emma spat at him. 'Why shouldn't I take it seriously? This is my *life*! It doesn't matter to you! We all know *you* don't take your job seriously. You didn't ask for it and you don't deserve it. The only time you show any serious interest is when you deal with the construction side of things. You can manage this company on your head but I don't happen to think that's good enough! Half the time when we're in meetings I get the feeling that you're not even here, that you're still mentally off building bridges——'

'Dams.'

She was brought up short by the terse rejoinder. 'What?'

'I only ever built one bridge,' he said evenly. 'I specialised in dams and irrigation projects.'

How little she knew about him. She couldn't possibly love a stranger! 'As far as I'm concerned you should have stuck to your speciality——' Instead of turning up here to ruin her life!

'Do I take that to mean that you would find it impossible to work as my executive director?'

Emma froze. After all the insults she had just heaped on his head, she couldn't believe she was hearing right. There was temper in his eyes, a good dash of it, but under control, unlike hers. 'You're offering me the job *before* I sleep with you?' she sneered with bitter sarcasm.

His eyebrows rose. 'If that'll make you feel better about accepting it. That way you and I at least can be certain it's not your performance in bed I'm judging you on.'

She almost choked on her outrage at his sardonic pronouncement. He was taunting her, he had to be... 'You know you can't do that... the board——'

'That's a crock and you know it. I'm running this company and if I want you, I get you.'

'But Sir Clive——'

'Clive will do anything to keep me here. Including giving me you.'

Emma laughed harshly. 'You still don't get it yet, do you? It's too *late*. I *can't* accept now. I couldn't bring any credibility to the job. People would say I'd only got it because I slept with you——'

'And are you happy to sacrifice yourself to a lie?'

'I have no choice——'

He swore fiercely, enraged by her stubborn pride. 'You little fool. Don't be so damned scrupulous. I'm giving you what you said you wanted.'

'Well, maybe I don't want it any more!' Emma yelled at him, hating him for making it sound like a beneficent gift on his part, rather than a reward for work well done on hers. 'Maybe I consider the price of working for an arrogant, selfish moron like you just too high! What you want is what you get. Well, this time, fella, you get zip!'

She slammed out of the office, surprising two secretaries frozen on a fascinated lean towards the panelled door. Halfway across the wide, open-plan clerical office that separated Frazer's suite of offices from hers his voice speared her in the back.

'Just what in the hell do you mean by that, Ms Rainer?'

She spun around and smiled viciously back across the sea of interested faces. 'It means, Mr Conway, that you can stuff your job. Donate it to some other charity! I *quit*!'

The blood was thrumming so loudly in her head that she didn't hear the blanket gasp, but her ears were burning by the time she dashed past Marc and collapsed back at her desk. She hadn't just burned her boats, she had immolated the entire harbour! And all because she had been shatteringly aware of a desire to fling herself into Frazer's arms and gratefully accept everything and anything he offered; to put her heart, her trust, her honour in his keeping, forever...

She felt a renewed surge of panic as she contemplated her actions of late. Making love in a cupboard and throwing a tantrum in the office! The Emma Rainer she had been a couple of months ago would never have *dreamed* of doing such things. She was changing, and she was very much afraid that the change was going to be for the worse!

Later, of course, logic returned with its comforting illusion of self-control, assisted by Marc's valiant efforts to agree that her outburst had been understandable, if not quite prudent. If she walked out now it would confirm all the ugly rumours. It would be giving Edward his mean victory on a silver platter. On the other hand, if she stayed, she would have to grovel to Frazer for her job back. She would have to bear the snickers, out-survive the rumours...treat what felt like a catastrophe as an amusing joke. And most definitely she would have to stay away from Frazer, otherwise there might be other nights, other cupboards...as far as Frazer Conway was concerned her resistance to temptation seemed to be nil!

Marc kindly left her alone when he was sure that her backbone was sufficiently braced and Emma stared at the phone on her desk with distaste. Could she bring herself to apologise? The light glowed on one of the internal lines and she snatched it up. Perhaps a legal problem—anything to take her mind off what she was going to have to do...

'Emma?'

'Frazer.' He didn't *sound* furious, but with Frazer it was hard to tell. Sometimes he could be smooth as cream and sharp as knives.

'Are you all right?'

'Fine.' She cleared her throat, and added more firmly, 'I'm fine.'

'Liar.' She heard the smile. It pinched her heart. Ah, Frazer, don't be nice... not now... I can't bear it...

'That was quite a show you put on.'

'Mmm.' A dangerous hum. The kind of hum that could go one way or the other depending on the response.

It was very cautious. 'You're not really resigning, are you?'

Emma gripped the phone tightly. 'I *should*...' There was dead silence from the other end and she sighed. 'There were an awful lot of witnesses...'

'You want them to bear witness to the fact that the Mouth Trap is a quitter?'

'Frazer——' He knew about that terrible nickname. Come to think of it he knew an awful lot of terrible, private things about her. If he wanted to he could blackmail her into staying...

'Emma.' The soft way he repeated her name soothed her feverish thoughts. 'I realise that your job is more important to you than anything else in the world. I don't want to be the one responsible for your losing it. And surely you're not going to let your dream slip away because of the actions of one arrogant, selfish male.'

'I... I shouldn't have said that——'

'But you did. And it was true. It's also true that Clive and I have very different perspectives on my role at ConCorp. He and I are very different people and I don't particularly enjoy having his greatness thrust upon me. I have plans, but they're not necessarily ones that Sir Clive will approve of. I need someone like you, trustworthy and loyal and utterly dedicated to the good of the company, to help me pursue them. Don't run out on me now, Emma, and don't let me push you out...'

'I...wasn't going to,' said Emma thickly, shattered by his sincerity. An hour ago she had been cursing his very name, and now here he was inexorably weaving himself back into her dreams. How did he do that? He made her sound vital to his survival. And he said that he knew that her job was the most important thing in the world to her. How lonely that sounded, put into such simple words.

She swallowed, took a breath and said shakily, 'Of course I'll stay. I...I lost my temper.' It stopped just short of an apology, but then she wasn't sure whether the situation warranted one.

There was a little silence. 'You sound funny. Are you crying?'

'No, of course not,' she said sternly, wiping the tears away.

'Of course not,' he agreed tenderly. 'After all, what is there to cry about? A bit of sorrow and strife never got you down before. You're a fighter, Emma, don't ever forget that again. Only—occasionally and for your own good—you should stop and make sure you know who you're fighting...and why...'

Oh, she knew all right. She knew exactly who and why. If Frazer put the slightest bit more pressure on her, she might crack, and then what? An affair? That would only compound her professional problems. Marriage? Even if he asked her there was only one possible answer. She had seen Frazer with his many great-nephews and great-nieces. She knew from Tom that he was a very loving father, in spite of the handicap of his frequent absences from home and hearth. Frazer had the looks of a quintessential swinging bachelor, but the spirit of a family man. Fatherhood completed him. He enjoyed it, needed it. Marriage to Frazer would mean babies, plural, for the woman who shared his future. Emma wouldn't let herself be trapped that way, not at any price.

And yet... was the alternative so greatly appealing? To be always alone, free... but to do what? To never quite trust anyone but herself? To be smarter, tougher, more independent and cunning than her male counterparts? She was twenty-six, and it occurred to her suddenly that she was still trying to live within guidelines that she had set for herself as a sixteen-year-old. What did a naïve, country-bred sixteen-year-old know of the world? A decade on she was a different person from the idealistic young girl who had thrown herself so eagerly into the freedom of university life. She had achieved many of those old goals, yet the challenge had always outstripped the sense of achievement. She had always felt that there was something more waiting for her, just out of her reach. She had never known exactly what it was. What more did she need in her life at age twenty-six that she hadn't needed at sixteen, or twenty, or even twenty-five...?

In the midst of her uncomfortable soul-searching Frazer suddenly decided that he didn't need to take up any more of her valuable weekends. He announced that he had found his preferred home and, with his customary decisiveness, sealed the deal with cash and moved in within forty-eight hours. Emma had silently smouldered when she discovered that the house was one of those they had looked at on the very first *day* of their search. She had loved it, but of course Frazer had found something to cavil about in every room, thereby confirming her conviction that their tastes, along with just about everything else, were completely incompatible. Now, with typical casualness, he had turned her conviction upside-down and shaken it out. Couldn't he *ever* run true to the form she had shaped for him?

Two days after his move into his new home, Frazer flew down to Wellington for a Construction Industry seminar and, deprived of his distracting presence, Emma rediscovered her misplaced confidence. She stopped imagining that every private conversation in the building was about her indiscretions, she haughtily out-sneered Edward, stoically weathered Charles Scott's heavy-handed disapproval and surprised Jasper by genuinely finding his *double entendres* more humorous than embarrassing. She even survived, without blushing, a visit to the office by Lady Conway and Tom, accompanied by the lovely, and very likeable Jenny Freeman.

Emma lunched with them, alert to every nuance of expression on Lady Conway's face, not daring to hope that Sir Clive hadn't told his wife about the closet incident. Even if he hadn't she must have heard about it through the very active family grapevine. However, it seemed Lady Conway was making no hasty judgements and, when she extended an invitation to dine a few nights later, Emma knew there was no way on earth she could refuse. Whether it was offered in ignorance or vindication, it was a chance to re-establish herself as one of the favoured few. She was too subtle to flaunt her invitation openly, but Marc made sure that the word was spread. The Mouth Trap was back!

She was slightly disconcerted, but not dismayed, to find it wasn't the formal/friendly dinner she had expected, but a family celebration at which she was the only 'outsider'. Sheena had discovered that she was pregnant—a glowing, relaxed Sheena whom Emma hardly recognised as the same woman. Steven, too, had a glow about him. He showed his newly callused hands with almost boyish pride and confided that he and

Sheena had almost resigned themselves to childlessness after years of trying.

'I guess the more uptight we got about it, the less likely it was to happen. But we've both been so preoccupied getting the new business set up that pregnancy was the last thing on our minds...the difference between unwelcome pressure and the kind that you enjoy, I suppose...'

Whether the family was being tactful, or merely preoccupied with the latest Conway development, no one mentioned Frazer except in passing. Not even Tom, who came to fetch her so that she could tell one of her now-famous stories to the mini-clan, freed from the dinner table to run riot in the playroom under Jenny's friendly direction. If performance rather than achievement was the standard of success in a job, then Jenny was every bit as successful as Emma.

'I hated school,' Jenny confided cheerfully, satisfying Emma's politely veiled interest as the children dashed around them. 'When it comes to formal learning, I bomb out completely, but then I never had any big ambitions so it didn't matter. A lot of the kids I went to school with got locked into dead-end jobs as soon as they graduated, just to make a living. Their whole life revolved around getting a pay-cheque and spending it at quitting time. They thought I was tying myself down but I figure I've got more freedom than they do. I'm pretty well my own boss—most of the time I please myself what I do and when I do it. Tom was a real easy baby and I used to tote him to tennis and the mall and the beach, and sometimes we used to travel with Frazer if he happened to be working somewhere civilised, so I got to see a bit of the world. As long as I kept Tom happy and the house clean and the meals coming—I love cooking—I was doing my job. Of course, when Tom goes to school it'll be different. I might think about doing some part-time nannying then, or maybe start a playgroup or something to do with cooking...'

Emma thought she had never met a more contented, well-adjusted young woman. No wonder Frazer trusted her. And despite her evident beauty she wasn't the least bit vain. She had had lots of boyfriends but none serious and that had suited her fine. Marriage wasn't a shiny trophy to be won but just something that happened if you were lucky enough to meet the right person. Emma envied her her uncomplicated beliefs and the bustling, happy atmosphere at the Conways prompted a sudden wistful longing for her own family, when she returned to her unnaturally quiet apartment. Despite the bickering, the unreal expectations, the great gulf of difference in education and outlook, her family was still her family. She didn't have to compete for membership, force a place for herself. She was Emma, she simply *belonged*...

Frazer was away for a week and, strangely, the huge ConCorp building seemed to lack something in his absence. His impact on the company had been subtle, rather than dramatic. His casual way of doing business, disconcerting at first, had quickly infiltrated the corporate consciousness, breaking down some of the barriers that had been created by a rigid hierarchy that had little real contact with the workers. Communication, once restricted to formal channels, was beginning to filter back and forth more casually and, where Emma would once have been horrified at being hailed by her first name by a clerk, now she shrewdly saw it as a sign of acceptance. It pleased her no end to notice that Edward still blindly insisted on being called 'Mr Cleaver' in respectful tones while Charles frequently answered to sir! Only she and Jasper took readily to the new trend of informality.

The day before Frazer was due back Emma had an early meeting with a consortium of investors to discuss a joint-venture mining operation. Her office had done the initial legal work on behalf of ConCorp mining and pin-pointed a number of areas which would require special clauses separating the company interests from the consortium's. Along with the general manager of ConCorp Mining and Jasper, who was handling the figures, Emma was empowered to negotiate an agreement, subject to the new clauses. The current uncertain economic climate had made the investors nervous, and Emma knew that this meeting was vital to engage their confidence. If ConCorp could land this one it would mean millions of dollars of extra profit each year, for at least the decade of the agreement.

So she was less than pleased at eight-fifteen in the morning, with a run in her tights and her hair still damp, to open her apartment door and find a frantic Jenny there, holding the hand of a flushed and sullen-looking Tom.

'I'm sorry, Emma, I really am, I hate to do this to you but I just have to go——'

'What's wrong?'

'Tom's sick and can't go to kindergarten and I have to go back to the States——'

'You *what*?' Emma backed away from the door as the two stumbled over the doorstep.

Jenny dropped a bulging duffel-bag on the floor. 'Tom's stuff is in there. I hate to do this to you—but I have a taxi waiting——'

'But—what is it? What's happened?'

'It's Tracey—that's my brother Andrew's wife—they got married last year—she's had a miscarriage and Andy's frantic. He's stuck in Dubai with no way of getting home for at least a week. He rang me and asked if I'd look after her and of course I couldn't say no, could I? Trace hasn't got any family of her own and the last thing she needs is to be stuck in hospital with no one to visit. I rang the airlines as soon as he called me this morning and I've got a flight out in——' she looked

at her watch and screamed '—forty minutes! God, I have
to go. Can I leave Tom? I'm afraid he's scratchy what
with being sick and all, but it's nothing too bad. I took
him to the doc yesterday and she said it's just a summer
cold, he doesn't have to stay in bed—there's some anti-
biotics in the bag, and the doctor's number——' She
was backing towards the door as she spoke, taking the
answer for granted. Emma was stunned.

'But...I have a meeting this morning—what about
Lady Conway——?'

'I phoned—I didn't get any answer. I couldn't wait.
Besides, Tom said he wanted to stay with you. Could
you try Aunt Dot later? Or Julie, or Miriam? Please—
I don't know what else to do!'

The normally unflappable Jenny was nearly crying and
Emma was suddenly disgusted with herself. First things
first: reassure Jenny, *then* panic!

'Of course I will. You go, Jenny. I'll look after Tom,
I promise. Don't you worry about a thing,' she said
firmly.

'Thanks.' Jenny fled gratefully down the hall. 'Tell
Frazer I'll ring from LA as soon as I know!'

As soon as she was gone Emma bundled Tom briskly
on to her bed so she could keep an eye on him while she
finished dressing. Tom immediately bounced off.

'Jen told you the doctor said I didn't have to go to
bed,' he said crossly. 'Can I watch TV?'

'It's too early for TV,' said Emma automatically. He
scowled, just like his father when he was thwarted. 'Have
you had your medicine yet?'

'Yep.' He and Frazer had invited themselves into her
apartment one morning when they had collected her for
the house-hunt but Emma had strictly confined them to
the ultra-neat kitchen and lounge. Now Tom indulged
his curiosity, poking about with a thoroughness that
again reminded her of his father. But Emma didn't have
time to linger. She left him to it and looked up Lady

Conway's telephone number. The first time she didn't get an answer, nor one from either of her daughters. She rushed away and wound up her hair into its customary knot without bothering to dry it first. Tom came and watched her skim on her make-up as she rang the first number again.

'What are you doing?'

'Putting on my make-up.'

'Are we going out?'

'*I* am. I have a meeting this morning.' At last, a click, and a hesitant voice. It was the daily cleaning woman. Lady Conway had already left for the island. She always went to Tiki Island on Friday mornings. And no, she didn't know where the other members of the family were—except for Mrs Sheena who'd gone with her mother-in-law.

Aware of the relentless march of time, Emma struggled into a new pair of tights and called Marc. He lived closer to the office than she and she hoped he hadn't left yet. He hadn't. When she sketched the situation, he switched into high gear.

'Do you want me to get a sitter from an agency?'

Emma might be grimly practical but she wasn't inhuman. She wasn't going to leave Tom with a total stranger. 'No. I want you to come over and stay with him.' She overrode all his spluttering protests smoothly. 'Trudy can take the notes at the meeting, and I'd rather have the comfort of knowing that Tom's in capable hands here. And don't tell me you couldn't cope...you've kept him perfectly amused at the office when he's had to hang around waiting for his father. He likes you, that's the most important thing...'

'I don't want Marc, I want you!' Tom burst out when she completed the call. 'You *have* to look after me. You told Jenny you would!'

'I know. But I didn't mean that I would stay home and look after you. This meeting——'

'But you can't go! You can't! You promised!' He looked as if he was going to cry. In fact he was. Big, fat tears were flowing out of his big blue eyes and down his adorable cheeks, seeping into his dimples. Emma's heart contracted and she gave him a hug and held him close, cooling his feverish skin with hers.

'Oh, Tom, don't cry...'

'Then you'll stay!' The tears seemed to vanish suspiciously quickly and Emma's own eyes narrowed.

'Tom, I told you, this meeting is very important——'

'More important than me?' he sulked.

'No. But important in a different way. I have responsibilities, Tom. I can't just shrug them off because you're sick.'

'I thought you were my friend. You said that you'd make time for me if I ever needed you, but you didn't mean it——' He threw her own words back in her face and screwed his face up self-pityingly. Emma knew she was being manipulated but couldn't help a fierce surge of guilt. If she was the kind of woman Tom and his father wanted her to be she would probably stay without a second thought. But she wasn't. Tom was a little off-colour and cranky as a result. He was an energetic, sociable little boy who would chafe at the restraints that even a slight illness imposed. He was also just a little bit spoiled by the attention he had been getting the past few weeks. He wanted to be amused and he had fixed on Emma to be the one to amuse him. Well, perhaps Tom was not too young to learn that the almost magical attraction that she had for children, him included, was not entirely of her own choosing. That although she loved children she wasn't a fairy godmother without feelings or needs of her own, ever available to grant his every wish. Her generosity had limits. Parents made sacrifices for their children but sometimes a child had to make sacrifices, too. Not that she was Tom's parent, but the principle was the same. She sensed that if she gave in too easily this time, it would set a dangerous precedent for the future, for both of them.

'Tom, darling...' She crouched down and smoothed back the tumbled curls, choosing her words carefully. 'If I thought you really needed me, of course I would stay. But there's a difference between wanting and needing and I think you're old enough to see it. I *want* to stay here with you. I don't want to have to go off and worry about you, but it's not as easy as just doing what you or I want. A lot of people rely on me to do my job properly. I'm proud of the respect that I've earned. I'm proud that people know that Emma Rainer is not going to let them down without a very good reason. If it were *me* who was sick, I would still go in to the office—that's how important today is to me...'

Tom's lower lip was quivering and Emma teetered on the brink of defeat.

'Tom, if you're really feeling bad and you really *need* me, then I guess that doesn't give me any choice,' she said desperately. 'But I have to be honest. I think you're trying to make me feel bad so I'll do what you want.'

'You hate me,' he said in a hard little voice. This time the threat of tears was genuine.

Instead of reassuring him, she questioned gently, 'If I *do* go into work, Tom, are you going to take away your friendship?'

He wanted to shout a sullen *yes*, she could see it in his eyes, but then they slid away from hers and he shook his head and whispered chokily, squeezing his arms around her neck, 'I love you, Emma.'

She had to hold back her own tears. 'Well, that means we're stuck with each other, because I love you, too.' She steadied them with her lovely smile as she said gravely, 'And I won't stop loving you just because we argue or hurt each other sometimes. It's not easy for me to have to say no, Tom, and to leave knowing that I'm disappointing you. Thank you for not making it harder than it already is. I'll be thinking about you and I promise I'll come back as soon as I can. OK?'

'OK.' He wasn't happy, but then, she wasn't expecting miracles.

He cried a little when she left but it was more of a plaintive wail of resignation than a full-blooded protest, and the colourful stack of cartoon videos that Marc had brought with him would no doubt soon prove a distraction.

Emma still felt a little guilty, but also sneakingly proud of the way she had handled a difficult situation... and proud of Tom, too. As proud as if he had been her own son!

CHAPTER NINE

'You're talking us round in circles, here, Dyson.' Emma tapped her silver pen impatiently on yet another counter-proposal that Trudy had just hurriedly photocopied and was distributing around the boardroom table. So far the consortium, led by a pugnacious Harold Dyson, had stonewalled her efforts to ease the terms of the original proposition. 'As I see it, our input requires a greater degree of physical commitment that should be reflected at board level——'

Emma was just getting into her stride when the door to the boardroom slammed open and Frazer Conway walked in. He wasn't wearing a suit and the designer stubble was back. He looked tired, crumpled and thoroughly out of place in the hushed boardroom. He also looked furious.

Emma, seated at the other end of the long, polished table, attempted to defuse the impact of his belligerent arrival by saying mildly, 'Frazer... we weren't expecting you back until tomorrow.'

'I gathered *that*,' he rapped tautly at her.

Emma was annoyed. Was he questioning her ability? 'Did you want to sit in on the meeting?' she asked, in a coolly discouraging voice.

'No. I want to speak to you, Emma. Outside.'

Emma couldn't believe her ears. He had spoken to her as if she were some lower form of life, not a respected colleague. She tried to cling to her professionalism.

'We're due to break for lunch in half an hour——'

'Now. I want to see you *now*.' The stony, slit-eyed mask slipped and showed a white-hot fury. A more pronounced ripple of unease travelled around the table. Frazer turned his head to speak to Trudy, but didn't take his eyes off Emma's rigid figure. 'Get coffee for everyone, Trudy. Take five, gentlemen. Ms Rainer will be back with you shortly.' The crisp statement didn't sound particularly reassuring.

Frazer put his hand on the open door and jerked his head at Emma. She rose, stiff with rage and embarrassment, and swept down the length of the room and past him without a glance.

She walked rigidly to the far end of the adjoining office, and spun around ready to attack, but he kept on coming, forcing her to hurriedly back up. 'I went round to your apartment. I thought you were supposed to be looking after my son!'

Emma's heart came to a sickening stop at his savage tone. 'Has something happened? Isn't he there?'

'Oh, yes, *Tom* was there! Very upset——'

A guilty, lurching heartbeat at his odd emphasis. 'You mean, Marc had *left* him——'

'*You* had left him!' The accusation was flung down like a gauntlet.

'But, didn't Marc explain——?'

'Oh, yes, he explained all right!' Frazer snarled. 'How after accepting responsibility for Tom you cheerfully dumped him because you couldn't be bothered——'

'I didn't dump him, and I certainly didn't do it cheerfully!' Emma stated flatly 'Is he still there——?'

'He's down in my car. I'm taking him home. I just wanted to hear your excuse in person——'

'I don't need an excuse, I have a perfectly good *reason*. You know how important this meeting is. And Tom understood...I told him——'

'Some garbage about how he didn't really need you, yes, so he said. How convenient for you.' The sarcasm was vicious. 'He's four years old! He may have intelligence beyond his years but his heart and emotions are still those of a baby! He's ill; the closest thing he has to a mother has suddenly disappeared and the person he turns to for comfort in his fright and bewilderment deserts him as well——'

'That is *not* the way it happened!' Emma's voice rose to combat the power of his cold fury, her eyes spitting fire to his ice at the injustice of his remarks. She had seen him angry before, but never like this. His tanned skin was pale, stripped of warmth, the strong angles of his face were hollowed with fatigue, the skin tight with a fierce tension that expanded his whole body into a solid wall of muscle. The lightweight cream shirt and trousers he wore seemed to barely contain his raw, physical aggression.

'He said you told him that you loved him. My God! Is that your notion of love? Whatever's expedient? Tom's not a toy, a cute interactive doll to be played with when you can spare the time and shoved carelessly back into the cupboard, out of sight and out of mind, when you have better things to do——'

It was unfortunate that he used the word *cupboard*. It triggered Emma's defence mechanism. 'I'm never careless,' she grated at him. 'You're deliberately being simplistic.'

'No one ever said loving was uncomplicated or easy. But it comes naturally to most people who aren't cringing away from the responsibility——'

'Don't talk to me about responsibility, you're stepping on to very shaky ground there, Frazer,' Emma warned him bitterly. 'I had to do my job but I didn't forget Tom. In fact I rang him during a coffee break a couple of hours ago. He seemed fine then——'

'Well, he sure as hell wasn't fine when I got there. He was crying——'

'You mean he cried when he saw *you*!' Frazer's eyes flickered briefly and Emma knew she had guessed right. She had enough experience of children to know how easily adult guilt could be manipulated, consciously or unconsciously, by a disgruntled child.

'The point is that you betrayed his trust. You showed him how little he means in your great scheme of life——'

'Why are you trying to make *me* feel guilty? I did the best I could in the circumstances. Why aren't you off ranting at Lady Conway, or your nieces, for not being available when they were needed? And what about yourself? How many times have *you* dumped your responsibility for Tom on to someone else for the sake of your job? You went away, too, remember. But, hey, you're a man, you're *important* . . . what you *do* is important! A man has the right to balance personal and professional demands sensibly. But a woman, a woman has to be soft and compassionate and always, but *always*, available!' Now it was Emma advancing, and Frazer in retreat. She was glad that she was wearing her most formal suit, a dark-blue pin-stripe with uncompromisingly powerful shoulders. She stood in the attitude of a victor, navy court shoes planted firmly and comfortably apart, hands on hips, chin high. So why did she feel as if she was losing? He was so right about love not being easy. Loving him was the hardest thing she had ever done.

'Tom wasn't sick when I went away——'

'And he's not sick now. He has a mild cold, that's all.' Emma's voice unconsciously softened now that he was on the defensive. 'You're over-reacting, Frazer——'

'Don't tell me how to act!' Frazer exploded furiously at her condescension.

'Then stop telling *me* how to act!' Emma matched him with equally swift fury. 'What I am has never been good enough for you, has it? I'm not very good at filling other people's shoes. I'm not your wife, Frazer. I'm nothing *like* your wife.' It hurt to admit it, to admit she wasn't good enough for him. She rallied, 'What is it exactly that you want from me? Do you even know? I don't! You wanted me to loosen up—I loosened up and it nearly cost me my job. You wanted me to hunt houses for you—then you make an arbitrary decision on your own. You want me to accept that we can mix business and pleasure without problems—and then you do something like this!'

With each angry word Emma felt a little more free, until suddenly she was soaring to the heady heights. It was a blessed relief to be suddenly too angry to care for anyone else's feelings. She glared at him.

'How dare you behave as if you own me? How dare you take me for granted? How dare you insult me for being myself instead of your unsullied fantasy of maternal sweetness and light? I told you I wasn't. Over and over I told you what was important in my life. But you didn't listen. You thought you knew better. You're no different from my family, or Phillip, or anyone else who assumes that I can be shaped to fill the gaps in *their* lives.

'Don't think I don't know why you kept pushing Tom and I together! Right from the first you used him to get to me. You tried to push me into "realising" where my true vocation lies. *Your* truth, Frazer, not mine. *Never* mine! You don't need me as a lover, let alone a wife—after all, how could I possibly measure up to the perfection of Sally? No, what you want is for me to be a *mother*. Once you knew about my affinity to children, that was all you saw. All you wanted to see. The rest of me didn't count for anything in spite of your fine words. Well, look again, Frazer Conway!'

He looked. She was magnificent: angry, proud, and remote...untouchable in her self-completeness.

'Now get out of here and let me do the job I'm being paid to do,' she scorned. 'And don't you ever, *ever* presume to usurp my authority like that again. All I want from you in future, Frazer Conway, is the respect due my position in this company, the respect you *owe* me. My life is *mine*. Find some other woman who won't mind stagnating as your hausfrau!'

The response was as swift as it was devastating. 'Other?' A mocking smile ripped from his lips. 'You're so busy thinking and acting and dressing like a man I wonder that you can still remember your sex. Maybe you'd like ConCorp to pay for the operation. Then no one will ever confuse you with a woman again——'

Emma had never struck anyone in her life. Words had always been her cudgels. Now she stared, stunned, at the marks on Frazer's cheek, white on white. Then the blood rushed into the fingerprints and Frazer's cruel, sardonic smile raised an answering blush of mortification on her stricken face as he said softly, remorselessly, 'But in some ways you still fight like a woman, don't you, Emma? Relying on my hypocritical, outdated gentlemanly instincts to protect you. You can relax. I don't hurt women, children or dumb animals. In fact I try not to hurt anyone at all. What a pity you're not "man" enough to say the same...'

Dyson and his team must have been taken aback at the tigress who rejoined them in the boardroom several minutes later. Gone was the cool, detached negotiator who patiently endured extended debate on each and every point, and in her place was a grim, implacable foe with a taste for blood. Dyson must have assumed that her sudden turnabout was the result of specific instructions from Frazer to play hard-ball to try and force the consortium to break off negotiations...perhaps because ConCorp had had a more favourable offer of funding, or had conducted its own secret geological studies that led it to reassess the profitability of the project dramatically upwards. He suddenly became much more amenable to ConCorp's suggestions, and by the end of the afternoon they had hammered out an agreement far more favourable than Emma could reasonably have hoped for.

But her personal pride in the achievement was tainted. If not for Frazer's untimely interruption, things might have turned out differently and, she suspected, a great deal less successfully. Once again, he had succeeded in sabotaging her supreme self-confidence.

Marc was at his desk when Emma and Trudy came down from the boardroom and, instead of giving the younger girl his usual smouldering smile, he looked uneasily at his boss.

'Uh...Frazer came by the apartment——'

'I know,' Emma said curtly. 'He called in here, too.'

Marc took off his glasses and fiddled with the frames. 'He didn't say much but he didn't look too happy.'

'You're a true master of understatement, Marc.' Emma's voice was as dry and gritty as her eyes. Frazer must have really unnerved her secretary. Marc, the unflappable, was almost twitching.

'I tried to explain but he seemed to think he knew all the answers,' he murmured, putting his glasses back on and studying her controlled expression. 'Did he blow his top?'

'Yes. And I blew mine.' Marc looked alarmed and Emma smiled grimly. 'And then I threw him out on his ear!'

Wisely Marc decided that he had been curious enough. He quickly got his head down with Trudy and they divided up the confidential tapes of the meeting to type between them.

With even greater tact, Marc made sure that for the tail-end of the day Emma was kept frantically busy, and it was only when she let herself into her apartment late that evening that she permitted herself to think about that awful scene with Frazer.

She had stood up to him, yes, but at what price? He now despised her as a cold, heartless automaton. She should be relieved. Now he would leave her alone. Now all her problems would melt away and everything would be the way it had been.

She had brought her usual briefcase full of work home, but just to look at it made her feel weary and hollow. She forced herself to eat a good dinner and still felt empty. She made a batch of biscuits. She tried to read. She ran a bath and wallowed in it for an hour, lecturing herself.

The trick was to convince herself that although, OK, she loved the wretched man; it was a love doomed from the start. He wanted too much, and so did she. They were so different—he free and easy, casually successful at apparently everything he did, Emma serious, guarded, intense, always having to struggle to reach her goals. And Tom. She could never have given Tom the kind of constant attention that Frazer thought he needed from the females in his life. At least, she could have, but it would have killed something in her, something of herself that was even more vital to her than love. Self-respect.

She was crying, she discovered in surprise, the steam from the bath mingling with the cool tracks of her tears. She wiped them away with the sponge and then gave up the trying to stem the tide. She deserved a good cry. She had earned it, damn it! She could have just grabbed what she wanted, thrown herself into an affair with Frazer and walked ruthlessly out on him when the relationship began to suffocate her, as it surely would. But no, instead she had made a sacrifice, for his sake, and for Tom's. Frazer had spoken of love...better that he be disappointed in her now than later, when the ties of love had had time to bind and cut too deep to loosen without agonising pain on both sides. If she felt this bereft now, how much more shattering a parting would be a few months hence, when the truth could no longer be ignored.

She felt better after her crying jag, drained but somehow refreshed. It felt good to wallow in self-pity for a change instead of pretending she was invulnerable.

After her bath she doggedly pampered herself with skin cream and exotic perfume. Instead of blow-drying her hair into its usual sleekness, she lay on the bed and hung her head off the edge and used the dryer to blow her hair into a thick, unbrushed blonde tangle. She looked at herself in the mirror. The wild, untamed style suited her reckless mood. She looked at her body. It was unfashionably pale because she had better things to do with her time than bake in the sun, but Frazer had seemed fascinated by its whiteness. No doubt he was more used to leathery California beach-bimbos, she thought cattily.

She smoothed a hand wonderingly down her side, from the swell of her breast to the flare of her hip. There was pleasure in knowing that she was different...unique, even if that uniqueness was part of what made them impossible as a couple. She knew that, whatever else was wrong between them, sexually she and Frazer would have been dynamite together; he had proved that beyond doubt. Her breasts ached at the memory of that secret, sinful session in the cupboard and she quickly turned away from the mirror, slightly horrified by her body's eagerness to over-ride her brain.

She found the long, thick, luxurious white towelling Givenchy robe, lapels and pockets piped elegantly in black, that she had treated herself to in a weak moment, and wrapped herself in its concealing folds. Then she checked the paper and her eye was caught by the late-evening movie. *Brief Encounter*. The original, not a glitzy remake. More tears, but at least this time they wouldn't be for herself. Or would they? The title of the movie did seem to rather suggest her fate. If she couldn't bring herself to trust any man with her happiness she would be destined to a lifetime of brief encounters.

She stacked up her pillows and puffed up her duvet and buttered the crackers and put a carton of milk in the silver ice-bucket that she had inherited from a favoured aunt for her hope chest. In her case it should be the faded hope chest, she thought wryly, as she opened a new packet of tissues and placed them on the Korean chest that doubled as a bedside table.

The first batch of crackers lasted through to the third commercial break. She had gone through several tissues already, in anticipation of tragedy, and her eyes were pink-rimmed as she took her plate out to the kitchen and on impulse this time added some Vegemite on top of the butter, using the salty dark spread generously. Vegemite and tears go very well together, she decided as she licked the spoon. Catching sight of her face in the reflective door of the microwave, she smiled reluctantly. With her hair erupting in violent tangles and a milk moustache adorning her upper lip she looked a million light years away from ConCorp's Mouth Trap. She looked more like a mad professor. A pity she couldn't madly invent a super-cure for a broken heart.

She was halfway back to her room when the phone rang. She detoured to the lounge to pick it up, and was surprised when she heard the voice.

'Marc?'

'Sorry to call so late. I...er...no one's there, are they?'

'No, I was just going to bed.'

'Oh.' He coughed. 'Well, maybe I'd better let you go——'

'Marc. Don't tell me you just rang to check up on whether I was having a wild party without you!'

'No. That is...it probably doesn't matter, but I just thought...if you'd had a fight...I mean, I know how you are about your privacy...you might not want——'

'Marc, what is it you're trying to say?' She was amused by his gauche stammering. This from Mr Smooth himself.

'Uh . . . you know that apartment key you gave me this morning? You know . . . for emergencies . . .?'

He paused, as if hoping she'd figure it out for herself. 'Yes?' Emma said encouragingly, her soggy brain not up to the challenge.

'Well . . . You see, we all left together and then Tom found he'd left his stuffed tiger behind and he was a bit weepy so . . . well, so I gave Conway the key to get back in . . .'

'And . . .?' She doggedly rejected the obvious.

'And he's still got it. I just thought I'd let you know. In case you want to bar the door or something.' He followed the weak joke with an even weaker laugh. 'Look, it's nothing, I just remembered, that's all and I thought . . . well, you never know what Conway's going to do. You can't call him predictable, can you? I'll get the key from him tomorrow so you don't have to worry about asking for it. Uh . . . why don't you just forget I called? It probably could have waited until the morning but I guess I wanted to cover my bases. 'Night, Emma.'

He rang off more quickly than was polite and Emma was still standing holding a dead receiver when she heard the dead-locked front door open. She stared with fatalistic calm at the door as she listened to steady, male footsteps. Frazer was all in black, which suited the funereal mood of the relationship, thought Emma numbly.

'If that's an emergency call you'd better call back,' he said carefully, wary of her attitude. 'They're not too keen on false alarms.'

'I . . . no, it was Marc. He . . . he just remembered about the key,' said Emma huskily. She dropped the receiver, not even noticing that she missed the cradle completely.

'I didn't think you'd let me in if I knocked.' When she didn't scream or throw anything, he prowled across the room and gently replaced the telephone receiver correctly.

'I certainly wouldn't have.' Emma tried to sound assertive and only managed to sound bewildered. She didn't know what to do. Why had he come? How had he known she wanted him to...?

Frazer's face, which had been set into sombre lines of determination, eased a fraction. 'So I saved us the bother of another futile argument. I would have got in eventually, you know. I'm nothing if not persistent. Here's your key back, by the way.'

Emma took it numbly. She should be angry. She should demand he turn around and walk right out again. Where was her pride? Her independence? She looked at him, mentally summoning a haughty frown. He had showered and shaved. His tanned jaw was velvet-smooth, the shaggy dark gold hair damp at his nape, and there was a crisp, fresh, masculine fragrance rising from the open throat of his black silk shirt. Recklessness ran like a river through her veins. Why not? Just one time... Why not be what he wanted...?

'I'd have brought you some flowers but I thought you might prefer the words,' he said, moving close enough to touch.

Emma swallowed, the plate in her hand tilting dangerously. 'What words?'

He tilted the plate back up with a finger. 'Is this dinner?'

'No, I...I ate earlier.' She didn't trust his soft speech. Where had all the blinding rage gone? 'I was just having a snack...'

'I'm glad I didn't spoil your appetite. I certainly ruined mine.' His smooth-throated voice soaked into her senses like mellow wine.

'W...What words?' she insisted, stubbornly resisting the sensual pull.

'I went off the deep end this afternoon for a whole lot of reasons,' he said, knowing it had to be said, speaking quickly, impatient for it to be over. 'I'd worked like the devil in Wellington so I could take off early and get back to you...and Tom——' This time it was his son who was the afterthought. 'I was dead tired and upset by the news about Tracey and worried by Jen's sketchy mention of Tom's illness. I suppose you could say I panicked.' He shrugged self-derisively at the admission. 'Not something I'm prone to do. The only bright spot was that Jen said *you* were caring for him. I raced straight round here desperate for sympathy and reassurance, brimming with gratitude, and found that beach-boy sidekick of yours in residence. For a moment I thought he'd moved in with you. He's lucky I didn't break his patrician nose.' He briefly contemplated the unreasonable satisfaction it would have given him. 'I felt...abandoned. And then Tom bawled his head off and I was sure he did, too. It was the last straw. I wanted to throttle you.'

'I noticed.' Emma's free hand crept up to her throat. Frazer absently followed the gesture, and then he seemed to notice the minutiae of her appearance. The blue eyes widened noticeably as they flicked down the length of the robe, then moved up over her hair, her pink eyes and her mouth. Did he think she looked a fright? He smiled suddenly, one of those tender, melting smiles that he reserved for special occasions, special people. He reached out and traced her upper lip and as she stood stunned by the feathery touch he transferred the finger to his mouth and tasted. His brow wrinkled.

'Milk?'

Another secret bit the dust! Emma rearranged the crackers into precise lines on the plate while she thought of something to say.

'Where's Tom?'

'With Miriam. She and Julie were on one of their shopping marathons today, that's why you couldn't get hold of them. I'm sorry you got mixed up in the mess, today of all days...'

Emma felt her eyes prickle anew. She counted the crackers carefully. 'Is he feeling better?'

'He's fine. In better shape than me, in fact,' said Frazer impatiently. 'Let's leave Tom out of this——'

'That's not what you said this afternoon——!'

'This afternoon I was terrified you had talked yourself back into your shell! Fear has its own language, most of it foul. I was afraid you'd decided that Tom and I were too much trouble...that I'd scared you off. For God's sake, Emma, I was hurting. I wanted you to know what you were doing to me!'

'It sounded more like a lecture to me,' she told him, and he shifted restlessly, unused to having to answer to criticism, however well deserved.

'I got confused,' he said sullenly. 'I saw you sitting there, cool as a cucumber and tough as old boots, and I thought "she's more comfortable here than she is with me". I knew I'd made a wrong move as soon as I saw your face but I couldn't stop myself. I had to save *my* face by saying it and I guess I let my insecurities do it for me. Tom was just the catalyst. It was either yell at you or throw myself at you in tears and beg you not to desert me, beg you to love me. Somehow, in the circumstances, I think you preferred the yelling. I hear you clinched the mining deal...congratulations.'

If he'd cried like a little boy there was no way she could have muscled her way back into that meeting and scuttled the opposition. The very thought sent cold chills down her spine. She stared at him. Had he really been that near the edge? Beg her to love him...? Hot chills chased the cold ones.

He was watching closely the effect of his words. 'You must know how I feel by the crazy things I've said and done since I've met you. You're like a drug in my system, Emma, every day I need more and more of you just to keep me functioning like a human being. I need to know that you feel something, too. You do, don't you, Emma? That's why you've been crying...your lids are all puffy. Were you crying for us, honey...?'

'Celia Johnson,' she said faintly.

'What?'

'I was crying for Celia Johnson. The movie. On TV.' He frowned and she gestured vaguely towards her bedroom. A mistake, for Frazer took it as an invitation. Or was it a Freudian slip?

He paused on the threshold, noting the muted television, the ice bucket, the milky glass, the crumpled tissues strewing the bed and the tumbled white sheets. Messy. He felt a surge of hope. His efficient Emma indulged herself in her bedroom. Perhaps she would indulge him, too. After all, she had let him get this far without too much trouble. 'You sleep in a double bed?'

'Queen-size,' corrected Emma, hovering behind him.

'It would be,' he said, with the first glimmer of real humour. He took the plate of crackers from her nerveless fingers and put them on top of the box of tissues, then he took her by the hand and led her over to the big bed and nudged her on to it. 'We'll watch the rest of it together,' he said, removing his shoes and stretching out beside her. 'I need something to take my mind off my troubles.'

Emma suspected what that something was going to be, and it wasn't an old movie! 'I meant every word I said this afternoon,' she warned, inching away from him.

He smiled at her. '*I* didn't,' he said kindly.

'You said I wasn't a woman——'

His smile drifted from sweet and innocent to sensuous and lazy. 'And you believed me? When you know you can turn me on with a look from those honey eyes?' He picked up the tie to her robe and toyed with it as he looked at the screen. 'The only time I have to hide my inclinations in closets, honey, is when I can't get you alone anywhere else.'

Emma blushed. Even if she could have picked up the threads of the plot she couldn't have concentrated on the movie, not when she could see from the corner of her eye that Frazer's absent twisting had loosened the knot in her belt. The soft towelling had already slid back to show a long length of thigh, and now the top was slipping over one shoulder. She should stop this right now!

She knelt and reached for a cracker and drank some milk, but it didn't help her concentration when Frazer watched her mouth move with all the intensity of a starving man.

'Frazer——' She tried to lick a crumb from her lower lip, but Frazer beat her to it. He half rose up, his tongue like warm, moist silk drawing across her skin. 'Frazer, we can't——'

'Are you still angry with me?' His breath whispered across her mouth, teasing it with promises. 'Perhaps words aren't enough, after all. Why don't you let me show you how much I appreciate you as a woman...?'

He lay back on his side, drawing her hand to the heart of him, then to the centre of his body, stroking her fingers around him. 'You see. I'm in your hands, literally as well as figuratively...be gentle with me.' He took his hand away and put it on her loosened belt. It came apart at his touch.

'Oh!' Emma's hand fell away from him, but didn't move to pull the edges of her robe together. It was too intoxicating to have him here, like a dream, a fantasy, healing all the wounds that reality had ripped open...

'Oh,' he repeated, with a softly mocking reverence. He brushed her gently rising breasts with the back of his hand, the slight roughness of hair and knuckles a ravishing friction. He trailed the heated brand across her belly and rested it heavily at the apex of her thighs.

'I . . . I don't know . . .' she lied.

'It's not a test, you don't have to prove yourself,' he said, watching her skin bloom to his touch, her nipples flower with longing as he stroked the satin between her legs. 'All you have to do to make love is to feel love . . . and you do feel it, don't you, honey, you feel it so *strongly* . . .' He reached up and slid a powerful hand under her wild mane of hair and pulled her down, not violently, but slowly, deliberately on to his mouth. His hand cupped her breast as it swayed forward. It filled and overflowed his palm and he arched his chest to brush it against the swollen tip.

Emma's knees trembled with the effort of holding herself up, away from him. But the feeling of his mouth searching hers, questing for the pleasure he knew was there, the soft abrasion of his silk shirt against her breasts was too much. She sank down, down, further and further, enveloping him, holding him, tasting and inhaling him, surrounding and surrounded by him. He stripped her robe from her back and threw it away with a single gesture of magnificent impatience and they rolled over on the bed, and the black shirt and jeans smothered the heaped elegance of the white towelling. Naked, Frazer was all heat and hardness and undulating muscle as he revelled in the differences between them, studying the way their bodies moved together, tantalising and taunting with his slowness until the last of Emma's self-consciousness vanished in a frenzy of frustration and she attacked him, pinning him to the bed, laughing deliciously when he swore at the razor-sharp cracker crumbs digging into his back. Retribution was swift as he reversed their positions with an ease that showed her that her dominance had been all part of his lovely game.

'Sadist——' she gasped as he ground her into the crumbs with the heavy thrust of his hips, and he growled deep in his chest, and then his hands moved, and his mouth moved, and he slid roughly, tightly, into her and just as swiftly became gentle, slow and teasing, then rough again in a way that excited her beyond anything she had ever known. It surprised her, given his seductive skill with words, that Frazer was such a silent lover, but he devoted himself fiercely, single-mindedly to his task, exhibiting a concentration that Emma thought hazily he rarely exercised anywhere else. Oh, yes...Frazer Conway was an explosively unexpected lover. Her lover. His body glistened in a light sheen of sweat, rubbing the musky aroma of his arousal into her flesh as he led, then followed, then led again, always holding back, waiting for her to catch up, then dashing off again, drawing her upward and onward, further and further out of herself with every impassioned thrust until the final relentless, storming convulsion that felt as if it would never, never end...

CHAPTER TEN

'So you see, Sir Clive, in the circumstances I have no choice but to withdraw my name from the list of candidates you're putting in front of the board.'

This was the worst interview of Emma's life. Even worse than the one she had endured as a law school graduate raw, untried, conscious of her minority status, and, as it had turned out, wretchedly naïve. What made it so much worse was the fact that Sir Clive was taking it all so calmly. Of course, Sir Clive didn't know the whole of it. Emma had glossed over quite a lot. For instance, in admitting that she was compromised by her 'intimate involvement' with his half-brother she hadn't told him that the intimacy had happened only last night . . . *all* last night . . . and well into the morning! She hadn't told him that she had behaved with all the restraint of a nymphomaniac just released from ten years of solitary confinement. She hadn't told him that she had ravaged Frazer into exhaustion and then crept out while he was still asleep to avoid the inevitable morning-after embarrassment, leaving only a carefully worded note to say she had some work to finish at the office. At least, Frazer wouldn't have been embarrassed; the man had demonstrated that *nothing* in the realm of human sexuality embarrassed him. But Emma was used to being in control of herself. She had been on a natural high last night; a dangerous combination of anger and sorrow and desire had combined to make her act recklessly out of character. Frazer might expect her to be like that all the time!

And then there was the question of where they went from here. Emma didn't know. She needed to think. So she had made a dash for the only place that she felt completely secure and in control: her office. There to reassess her options.

If Sir Clive had gone to Tiki Island with his wife instead of delaying his weekend in order to invite a couple of old cronies for Saturday brunch in the company's penthouse apartment he might never have known the extent of her fall from grace. Their running into each other in the ConCorp lift was fate and she had rashly decided to meet it head on. Get it over with. She had gone up to the penthouse with him and there stumbled through an unrehearsed version of her surprise decision. But Sir Clive hadn't looked surprised. Instead he looked almost...*entertained*...by her stiff-upper-lipped confession.

'So...I take it you're not offering to resign altogether...?'

Emma jerked upright. *'No!'* Frazer might have snaffled her heart from her breast but he damned well wasn't having her job, too. She had been through that trauma once, for a pale imitation of the love she felt now, and once had been enough!

'Good. Good.' Sir Clive patted his pockets and drew out a cigar. Emma, not at all herself, gave it such a look of fierce, unadulterated loathing that he hurriedly put it back. 'Ah...it is of course a problem—men and women working closely together. Never had this trouble in my day, you know, but times change...times change.' His eyebrows beetled and he barked, 'Frazer's a good man. Stubborn. Knows what he wants and goes for it. A good father. Handsome, too. Got plenty of chances to play around but was never much interested.'

Emma's mouth tightened. Was he accusing her of seducing Frazer against his will? Of being a man-eater?

Frazer had certainly played around with *her*. She blushed as she remembered just *how* he had played around. She got even hotter when she recalled that she had done her fair share of man-eating. To her embarrassment Sir Clive's eyes twinkled as if he knew what she was thinking.

'Well, it's your decision, Emma. But maybe you'll change your mind when I tell you that the job's yours if you want it. Providing, of course, that you and Frazer stop all this pussy-footing around. It all has to be seen to be on the up and up.'

For one blind moment Emma wanted to leap up and say she'd take it. All she had to do was reach out her hand and everything she had ever wanted was hers.

Not quite...

She unclenched her fingers and studied her white knuckles. She would never forgive herself if she did that...threw over whatever hope there was of building any kind of personal future with Frazer for the sake of a hollow crown. She shook her head. One couldn't have everything. Life was a matter of making choices based on your own instinct for what was right. Frazer was wrong for her but this choice was a matter of pure faith and hope...

She took a deep, steadying breath. 'There'll be other chances for me. All I'm doing is postponing this one. I wouldn't be here if I didn't believe in that, believe in myself,' she said proudly.

Sir Clive's finger twitched without a cigar to roll. 'Mmph!' The grunt seemed to indicate approval. 'Not short of arrogance yourself, are you? Just to show there's no hard feelings, why don't you stay and have a drink? You ought to meet Doug Harmon. He's in natural gas. And Josh Mason is with the treasury department. Both could be good contacts for you...'

'I...was going to get some work done,' said Emma weakly, not daring to reject the olive-branch out of hand.

But it seemed that Sir Clive had the whole tree in mind. He ignored her feeble protests and set her up with the biggest brandy she had ever seen.

'Put a bit of colour in your cheeks, Emma,' said Sir Clive, finally lighting his cigar. 'Took a lot of guts to do what you've just done, to be that honest.' He chuckled through a cloud of smoke. 'Admire you for it. Lot of men would look a lot sicker than you do if they were asked to exhibit as much principle. It's a real pity, though...that you couldn't keep your hands off my brother.'

Fortunately his guests arrived before Emma stopped choking on her brandy and Sir Clive insisted on another drink, and praised her to an embarrassing degree, linking her so often to Frazer and treating her with such bluff camaraderie that Emma was sure that the 'good contacts' got a very mistaken idea of her importance at ConCorp.

It was only after her third double brandy that she was able to extricate herself. Her head was so thick she knew there was no point in going back to her office and trying to think sensibly.

She did stop off, however, to ring her apartment. No answer. She felt a surge of relief accompanied by an equal surge of dismay. She should never have run out on him like that. Had he been angry when he found her gone? Had he found the terse note? She hadn't dared sign it 'love, Emma' because that would have been too much like a confession. The words had seemed to come all too easily to his lips, but from her they would be a promise that she still wasn't sure that she could ever keep.

She was feeling very jittery by the time she got to her car and she frowned at the keys in her hand. It would be just her luck to be stopped by a traffic officer and have to blow in a bag. Three double brandies on an empty stomach would have undoubtedly put her past the safety limit.

On the principle that anything that could go wrong would go wrong, Emma took a taxi home. Halfway there she changed her mind and gave the driver Frazer's new address. Brandy ran like fire in her veins. What was done was done. It was time to look forward, not back. Time someone *else* started making a few sacrifices!

The house was modern but built with an old-fashioned solidity and style, in a U-shape around a raised, timber-decked pool. Plain red brick was contrasted with grey shingles and big north-facing windows made every room warm and sunny. It was a house with character, cared for with obvious pride by its previous owners. The entryway was grey slate and Emma's heel tapped nervously as she waited for the doorbell to be answered.

Tom's expression when he opened the door to her was first delighted, then wary as he remembered.

'Hi, Emma.'

'Hello, Tom. How are you feeling today?'

'OK.' He sniffed to show her, still cautious.

'Am I forgiven for yesterday?' Emma smiled.

'Dad got real mad at you, didn't he?' said Tom solemnly.

'He thought I should have stayed home with you, instead of getting Marc to do it.'

'Marc was nice,' Tom offered placatingly. He sniffed again. 'Dad didn't come home all last night.'

'Really?'

Emma could feel her own skin getting hot under that innocent gaze. Although, maybe it wasn't so innocent after all because suddenly Tom grinned, his dimples winking. 'He was with you, wasn't he?'

'I . . . uh . . .' What was the etiquette in these cases? Should she leave Frazer to answer those wide-eyed questions? 'Is he in?'

Tom shook his head. 'He was a couple of hours ago, but then he went out again. He said he had to go in to work.'

Emma's heart plunged wildly. He had followed her. 'Was he...uh...in a good mood?'

Tom tipped his head on one side. 'He was *real* nice to the new nanny...'

'New nanny? I thought your—Miriam was looking after you.'

'She was, but George is sailing in a race today and she didn't want to take me 'cos of my cold and when Daddy didn't come home she got Trixie 'cos Aunt Mirry said Trixie is a treasure. She came round this morning. She's fun...but not as good as you,' he added hurriedly when he saw Emma's expression.

'Trixie?' It sounded like the name of a circus dog. Certainly not the name of a reputable nanny.

'Hello. Can I help you?'

Emma's jaw dropped. She had thought that Jenny was an attractive woman but this one left her for dead. Masses of midnight hair, eyes as green as emeralds, flawless skin and a figure to shame Miss World.

'This is Emma,' said Tom helpfully when it appeared that she had lost her voice.

'Oh. *Emma.*' A sexy, rose-pink coloured mouth curved knowingly as she and Tom exchanged smiles. Emma's blood-pressure shot up even further. This was a total stranger grinning as if she knew all about the mess Emma had so far made of her love-life. A total, *beautiful* stranger, proposing to live with Emma's lover. 'What are you keeping her on the doorstep for? Come on in. I'm Trixie.'

What did she expect—a fanfare? Emma regarded her sourly. Now, don't jump to conclusions, she told herself. Remember what happened last time.

'Not Trixie *Conway* by any chance?' she asked.

Even her laugh was sexy. 'Oh, Frazer and I aren't married, if that's what you're worried about!'

'I just wondered whether you were some relation of the family,' she persisted hopefully.

'Oh, no. I came through an agency.'

'You're a professional nanny?' she asked, just to make absolutely sure. 'You do this all the time?'

'Oh, no, only part time. To help pay for my studies.'

Oh, God, beautiful *and* intelligent. 'What are you studying?'

'Mechanical engineering. Come through to the kitchen and have some afternoon tea...'

Engineering? That settled it! 'I'm afraid there's been a mistake,' Emma said firmly as they entered the gleaming white kitchen that Emma had fallen in love with when they viewed the house.

'Coffee?' said Trixie amiably. 'What kind of mistake?'

'About your employment.'

'Oh, I know it's only temporary——'

More temporary than you know, vowed Emma silently. 'Frazer only wanted you to stay until I got here.'

Trixie's gorgeous brow wrinkled. 'That's not what he told me.'

'Frazer is very forgetful sometimes. It's his age. You know...male menopause,' she said spitefully. 'He told me to give you your wages——' Emma opened her handbag.

Trixie grew even more puzzled. 'But he knows the agency sends a bill——'

'This is a bonus. Compensation for the short term of your employment and thanks for helping out in a crisis,' Emma improvised, stuffing a wad of notes into the girl's reluctant hand.

'But, Emma, Daddy said Trixie was going to——'

'Tom!' Emma's voice rose just high enough to treble his. She cleared her throat. 'Tom, do you want me to look after you or not?'

'You mean, live with me and Daddy? Forever?' His little face creased into seams of satisfied smiles.

Emma wasn't quite ready to cope with the terrifying details. She turned her attention back to the gorgeous Trixie, who was counting the notes that Emma had given her. Mercenary tramp!

'Now, Trixie, I think it's time you went back to your studies,' she ordered.

'But ... I was making a casserole for dinner——'

'I can cook. And clean. And sew. And garden. And look after children. I am also a fully qualified lawyer and an executive with ConCorp. Anything you can do, honey, I've *already* done better!'

'Including sleep with the boss ...'

Emma spun around at the insolent drawl from the doorway. Frazer stood there, or rather, leaned there, arms crossed over his chest. He was breathing slightly fast and there was a faint glisten of sweat in the hollow of his throat where his knit shirt was thrown loosely open, but otherwise he looked totally relaxed—and revoltingly pleased with himself!

'What's going on here?' he asked, on the heels of his show-stopping remark.

'She was trying to throw me out.' Trixie pointed cheerfully at Emma. 'She said you told her to pay me off.'

'Did I tell you to do that, Emma?' Frazer taunted, revenging himself for a very long and fraught morning as he watched her flush with temper. Emma in a rage was as exciting as Emma in a passion, and just as vulnerable.

Emma's eyes narrowed to gold slits, knowing that he was riding her but unable to conquer her desire to explode very messily all over the kitchen. She knew it was ridiculous to be jealous when it was obvious that it was *her* that Frazer was chasing but she couldn't help it. That was the great thing about jealousy. It didn't have to be *reasonable*. 'Either she goes, or I do,' she gritted savagely.

Frazer settled himself more securely against the open door. 'Hmm, that *is* a poser.' He looked from one woman to the other, as if he were a sultan inspecting his choices for the night.

'Frazer——' Emma's voice was quiet with thunder.

'Frazer——' Trixie's was filled with amusement, but then she wasn't hopelessly in love...

'I'm thinking, I'm thinking...' he said blandly, his eyes dancing. 'Did she tell you she's going to be an engineer, honey?' he murmured to a simmering blonde volcano.

Emma exploded. She took Trixie by the slender, exquisitely tanned arm and showed her the front door—open. 'And don't come back!' she snapped.

'At least, not for an hour or so,' said Frazer, pushing Tom out of the door after Trixie. 'You and Tommy drive over to the playground.'

'But, Dad, I want to stay and watch!' his son wailed.

'Believe me, Tommy, you'd find it a yawn. You have a healthy disrespect for mushy stuff.' His father grinned. 'Here are my keys, Trixie, take the Ferrari. And here's some money.'

'It's OK. Emma gave me some cash,' said Trixie jauntily, grinning back at him, and winking at an offended Emma. 'See you two later. We'll toot when we come up the drive to warn you we're back!'

'You're letting her drive your Ferrari?' Emma demanded furiously. Knowing how men felt about their cars, she felt it was practically the equivalent of a wedding ring. 'Hadn't you better give her a test drive first? Or have you already given her one?' she added nastily.

'Come inside, darling, before you have apoplexy on the lawn.' Frazer tugged her back into the house. 'I told you, it's only a car. You can drive it whenever you like, I'm not possessive about things...only people.'

Emma was only partly mollified. 'Why did you hire her?' she demanded as he steered her into the large lounge. The colour of the carpet, she noted inconsequentially, was almost the exact shade of Frazer's eyes. Perhaps that was why he had bought this particular house. It suited his arrogance.

'I didn't. Miriam did.'

'Then why did you let her stay?' she said sullenly.

'Because she's unutterably gorgeous?'

'Get serious, Frazer!'

'Because I admire her brain?'

Emma's snort told him what she thought of that suggestion.

'Sexist!' He let her go and sprawled on to the black leather couch that ran along one wall, watching her move restlessly around the room. 'Would you believe because I was desperate? You'd disappeared and, knowing you, were intent on being stupidly proud and disgustingly practical and doing something that we'd all regret later. Trixie turned up at the moment of maximum panic. I just grabbed her.'

'I'll bet you did,' snarled Emma.

'Emma, stop it. You know you're not really jealous of Trixie, you're just using it as an excuse.'

'Don't tell me what I'm thinking——'

Frazer sighed and, as she paced past him for the third time, reached out and pulled her into his lap. He caught her flailing arms against his chest and wedged her head into his shoulder so that he could kiss her thoroughly.

She was gasping when she surfaced.

'That's the good-morning kiss that you denied me this morning,' he said huskily. 'Have you any idea how I felt when I woke up alone? I thought I'd dreamt it all...except I was in your large and lovely bed, and I ached in places a man only aches when he's overreached himself with an insatiable woman...'

Emma squirmed and a blissful expression crossed his face. She froze as she realised why, the thin fabric of her summer skirt even less of a barrier than the soft, well-worn denim that cradled his loins.

'I loved having you fight over me, honey,' Frazer purred. 'But you'll never have to worry about my straying. I'm a one-woman man and you're the woman. First I wanted you, then you taught me to need you. You see, I *do* know the difference. And I know a good marriage requires both, in their season. You need me, too, honey, that's why you tried to throw Trixie out. But unlike me you're afraid of being vulnerable. Don't be. Everything will be fine, you'll see...the four of us will make it work...'

'*Four* of us!' Emma struggled. 'Frazer, if you're talking about marriage because you think I'm pregnant you're being ridiculous. We only made love last night. And you used protection——' They toppled lengthways on the couch with the momentum of her struggle and Frazer seemed satisfied with this new angle on things. He wedged her against the back of the couch with a hard thigh pinned between her legs.

'I meant you, me, Tom and Jen—or Trixie, or whoever the current nanny might be.'

All Emma's doubts flared back into life. 'I thought you wanted *me* to play nanny,' she said stiffly. 'After all, you obviously don't see me having much of a future with ConCorp. I saw Sir Clive this morning and——'

'I know. You weren't in your office and then the security guard told me he'd seen you in the lift with Clive so I went up and had a very instructive chat with him—informative on both sides, I might add. I *knew* you'd do something stupid if I didn't reach you in time. Why in the hell did you go to the office at all?'

'Because I wanted somewhere to think!'

'You would have been better off discussing your thoughts with me——'

'Why? Because you're a man and I'm only a silly woman?'

He kissed her fierce mouth. And kissed her again when she swore at him. And kissed her again when she kissed him back.

'Because you're *my* woman and I'm your man. Any problems we have are mutual ones. Any support we need we can ask from each other. Honey, if you would only talk to me, tell me what you need instead of being defensive about it, maybe you'll find that we aren't as incompatible as you seem determined to think. What do you want, Emma?'

She looked at him. Looked at the intense blue eyes, the shockingly handsome face, the thick blond hair falling silkily across her hands which had somehow become linked around his neck. His heart was pounding against her breasts, his hips pushing hers into the button-backed leather.

'Everything,' she admitted sadly. 'I want it all. I want my career and I want to be loved and married and have children and still be free to be myself, and I...I...'

He leaned his hard forehead against her narrow one, his hands lightly cupping her waist as if he feared that to hold her harder would be to let her slip away. His silent urging gave her the courage to declare herself.

'I...want it with you. I want it all with *you*,' she tore the words free and scattered them to the fates.

'Oh, God, you don't know how long I've waited to hear you say that...' he told her thickly, suddenly trembling with an intoxicating relief. 'You can have it, honey, all that's in my power to give you. It took you a long time to realise it, but all you ever needed to do was *ask*.'

'But, Frazer, I can't,' she said, loving him for trying. 'I mean, it's a nice dream, but no one gets everything that they want. I know you won't be getting exactly what *you* want——' He put an imperious finger across her mouth, stopping the words.

'Who told you that?'

'Nobody. They didn't have to. I . . . I know most of the women of your family don't have jobs outside the home——'

'You're not most women. You're *the* woman,' he reminded her passionately. 'That's why I told Clive to forget he'd ever seen you this morning. To make nothing official until he got your notice of intention in writing——'

'It was *my* decision, Frazer,' Emma was quick to read an infringement of her rights. 'I won't let it be said that I slept with the boss, or even married the boss, for any other reason than . . . than . . .'

'Than that you're madly in love with him and can't live without him. I'm flattered, darling, but the fact is that the gossip might very well go the other way.'

'Whaa——?' Emma was dumbfounded by his lack of logic, her mouth shaping a small, soft oval of disbelief.

'Mmm.' Frazer traced the oval with his tongue and then inserted himself between her teeth, sliding into her moist depths. 'You taste of liquor . . .' He tasted again, at leisure. 'Brandy. The best, if I'm not mistaken . . .'

'Your . . . Sir Clive . . . he made me have some. I . . . I guess if I hadn't I wouldn't have come here and acted like . . . like . . .'

'A woman crazed with jealousy? That's not alcohol, that's love. Damned Clive! He just can't resist meddling. You'll have to clip his wings, darling, when you're in charge...'

Emma was interested in what his mouth was doing to hers, and what his hands were doing to the pearl buttons on her blouse. It took a few minutes before his words penetrated to her sluggish brain.

'What did you say?'

'Ouch!' Frazer touched his bitten tongue to his lips and smiled ruefully at her flushed face. While her mind had flown to business her body was defiantly out to lunch. He could see the stiffened points of her breasts thrusting against the cream silk of her blouse, and her legs were wrapped captivatingly around his. That she could be like this and still think straight was a tribute to her mental capacity. His was rapidly degenerating, but he knew that this was definitely a case where business must precede the pleasure he hoped would last the rest of their lives.

'I said, people will probably accuse *me* of manipulating *you* because I knew I didn't have the nous to run ConCorp myself. They'll say I manoeuvred you into marriage so that I could ally myself with the real power behind the company...'

'What on earth are you talking about?' She smiled at his babble.

'I'm talking about you running ConCorp. I'm talking about the fact that I don't, and never did, want to run the company by myself. I'm an engineer. I like being an engineer. It's my ambition in life—apart from being married to you. I'm quite happy to run the heavy construction side of ConCorp's operations but I don't want to be bogged down with the whole kit and caboodle. Sir Clive was always adamant that no one but family was going to control the company but his options were limited. We're just about to present him with another option, the only real option he has left. My wife. Emma Rainer Conway.'

Emma reared up on braced arms, stared down at him as if he had gone mad. He smiled tenderly, brushing back a strand of icy hair, tucking it behind her neat ear. 'You were right about me not really caring about the business. It's too big, too diverse for me. I like to concentrate my skills, to be a big fish in a little pool. It's what I want, Emma, and giving you what you want will coincidentally give me what *I* want. *Exactly* what I want. A job I love and a woman I love all in one fell swoop. You *have* to accept it, Emma, because it's your fault I even got involved in ConCorp in the first place——'

'What do you mean?' Emma still held herself over him, as if afraid that by touching his body she might contaminate her own with his madness.

'I mean the only reason I agreed to Clive's wretched scheme for making me his successor was because it gave me a chance to get close to you. I came back here for Tom, and to start my own engineering consultancy, full stop. There was no question that I was going along with Clive's attempts to sucker me into a job I knew I didn't want. Until I saw you. Clive told me when he was still trying to con me into replace Steve that he intended to give you the promotion but he wanted to "test your mettle" by seeing how you coped with the pressure of competition.'

'Why, the——!' When Emma remembered the hassles that she had gone through, all for nothing!

'Quite. So I had no qualms about playing along with him for my own purposes. I knew you were something special, even when you were spitting insults at me. I wanted to know you, I wanted you to know me, and I knew you wouldn't even let me get a foot over the threshold unless I had a lever to keep the door open. I told him last week that I intended to marry you and offer you more than just a ring. He was furious, not so much at my plans but at the fact that they weren't his, although the way he dangled you under my nose to begin with I'm beginning to have my suspicions...'

'No wonder he was so chirpy this morning,' said Emma sourly. 'I suppose he thought it was all a big joke.' She really should be annoyed with Frazer, too, for the shameless way he had manipulated her, but how could she complain at the result?

'Only to salvage his pride. He's already effectively transferred most of his power to me. All he can do is sit back and enjoy the ride. Now *you* get to pick who gets promoted. I've recommended Jasper. He's clever and young enough to be malleable. *And* he makes Clive nervous!'

'I think getting the better of Clive gives you more of a thrill then getting me does,' said Emma drily.

Frazer's mouth curved. 'You think so?' He exercised his strength and pulled her down hard against him, forcing her to straddle his hips. 'Honey, thrills like those we give each other aren't ten a penny.' He undulated his hips to give her the proof.

'Frazer——!' Her protest was less than half-hearted.

'You're the boss, Emma,' he growled wickedly against her throat. 'Tell me what to do and I'll do it. I can be *very* obedient when it's a beautiful woman ordering me around...'

Emma laughed. It was crazy! *He* was crazy! Could the answer to their problems really be this easy? Her laughter died.

'And what about children? I know you want more children...'

'Would you like to bear a child of mine?'

There was pride in her eyes as she relaxed against him. 'Yes.'

'Then have one, or two, or whatever. And Tom and I can help look after them. And Jen until she changes her mind. If and when she leaves we can get some other suitable——'

'Raddled old hag——'

'Comfortable, grandmotherly type,' he corrected her in amusement, 'to do the honours. You're the one with the rigid ideas about child-minding, not me. As long as our children are well-loved, darling, they're not going to lack for anything just because their mother has another kingdom to run. They'll be as proud of you as I am. And don't forget that we have a very fine extended family who are *usually* available to stick their oars in—in fact as you know they'd rather put a galley ship to shame.'

'I can't believe it's all that simple. You told me that loving was never simple,' whispered Emma, still dazed by the implications of what he had told her.

'But then, you don't like things to be easy,' Frazer pointed out in loving amusement. 'You enjoy a challenge. Well, honey, this may be your greatest challenge yet. I promise I won't expect a superwoman as long as you don't expect a superman. I'm offering you the deal of a lifetime, Emma. How can you turn it down?'

She looked at him. She couldn't. If there were loopholes in this marvellous proposal of his she no longer wanted to find them. She wanted to believe. She wanted to share his conviction that they belonged together. She smiled.

'Ahhh,' he sighed with a deep, masculine satisfaction. 'Have I ever told you how much I love your mouth?'

'I believe you may have mentioned it a few times last night,' Emma teased. To her disappointment Frazer suddenly rolled out from under her and stood. She got up reluctantly, her skirt askew and her blouse partly unbuttoned. She didn't bother to tidy herself up. She liked the way he was looking at her disarray.

'There's just one thing that I've really wanted to do, ever since I first met you,' he said, opening the glass doors that led to the sunbaked deck.

'Really?' she said, intrigued as ever by his unpredictable mood changes.

He took her hand and led her out by the sunlit blue waters of the pool. The sky above was equally blue. It seemed everywhere she looked the world was determined to remind her of Frazer's eyes. They were looking at her now, full of daring, and she suddenly backed away, beginning to laugh and shake her head.

'Oh, yes. It's what you deserved, you know, talking down to me the way you did...'

'No, Frazer, please. This is my best skirt, and the blouse is silk. *Frazer!*'

He picked her up by the waist and tossed her, catching her with an ease that made her feel as light as the breeze that ruffled his sun-gold hair.

'Frazer, please, I'll do anything you want——'

The water was warm satin on the surface and crisp in the watery depths. Emma surfaced spluttering, to see Frazer stripping off his shirt, jeans and briefs. He was stunningly male and deliciously unselfconscious as he dived in to join her.

'Damn you, I said I'd do anything——'

His sun-tanned face was slick, his eyes slitted against the glare, his mouth hungry. 'I know, and what I want is for you to make love to me in a swimming-pool. It's been a fantasy of mine since that first day, when you looked down your nose at me so haughtily. I wanted to push Her Haughtiness into the pool and watch those prissy clothes plaster erotically against her body and then peel them off...slowly...and float us both to paradise and back...'

As the waters closed over her head, Emma gave up the fight to preserve her dignity. There were times when it behoved the boss to let an employee have his way. And this was obviously one of them...the first, she would ensure, of many!

Harlequin Presents®

Coming Next Month

#1463 THE WEDDING Emma Darcy
Tessa has a wedding to call off and in her emotional state, she's not ready to cope with the unwanted attentions of the devastatingly handsome managing director, Blaize Callagan. First, he maneuvres her into becoming his temporary secretary, and then insists he become her groom.

##1464 SOME KIND OF MADNESS Robyn Donald
Alick Forsythe is exciting, dangerous—and already engaged. Laurel has had it with that type of man. But when Alick makes it clear that he's interested in her, Laurel's defenses begin to crumble. She knows getting involved would be madness!

#1465 SILENCE SPEAKS FOR LOVE Emma Goldrick
Brian Stone quickly hires Mandy Small as his secretary—he's impressed by the idea of someone who won't answer back. Then he proposes, but Mandy isn't sure of his reasons, and there is no way to tell him how she feels!

#1466 THE GEMINI BRIDE Sally Heywood
After being accosted in the street by a handsome stranger, Emma discovers that she has a double—glamorous TV presenter Cosy. It's quite a coincidence because Emma has always envied Cosy. But when Brick Dryden, a very charming yet arrogant man, suggests that she take Cosy's place, it makes Emma think twice....

#1467 HEART OF FIRE Charlotte Lamb
Claudia knows working for dynamic businessman Ellis Lefèvre will be a challenge. When he locks her in his hotel suite to type a confidential report, she begins to have real doubts about her boss and his unusual working methods. And those doubts are rapidly confirmed....

#1468 ROMANCE OF A LIFETIME Carole Mortimer
After a disastrous marriage, Beth isn't sure she wants to get involved with attractive Marcus Craven. They'd met by chance in Verona, but when he single-mindedly pursues her to Venice and from there back to England, she begins to question whether she dare fall in love again.

#1469 THE GIFT OF LOVING Patricia Wilson
Lucy has never met a more rude and insensitive man than Comte de Chauvais, and when her aunt accepts an invitation to stay at his château, Lucy is filled with foreboding. Will she be able to escape from the trap he has set—and the desire he arouses in her?

#1470 SICILIAN VENGEANCE Sara Wood
Smooth Sicilian Vito Velardi might be silver-tongued, but Jolanda knows he's dangerous. He'd made her father's life a hell, turning his own son against him, and Vito would hurt Jolanda, too. This time, she's determined to be the one pulling the strings..

OVER THE YEARS, TELEVISION HAS BROUGHT
THE LIVES AND LOVES OF MANY CHARACTERS INTO
YOUR HOMES. NOW HARLEQUIN INTRODUCES YOU
TO THE TOWN AND PEOPLE OF

One small town—twelve terrific love stories.

GREAT READING...GREAT SAVINGS...AND A FABULOUS
FREE GIFT!

Each book set in Tyler is a self-contained love story; together, the
twelve novels stitch the fabric of the community.

By collecting proofs-of-purchase found in each Tyler book, you can
receive a fabulous gift, ABSOLUTELY FREE! And use our special
Tyler coupons to save on your next TYLER book purchase.

Join us for the fourth TYLER book,
MONKEY WRENCH by Nancy Martin.

*Can elderly Rose Atkins successfully bring a new love into
granddaughter Susannah's life?*

"GET AWAY FROM IT ALL" SWEEPSTAKES

HERE'S HOW THE SWEEPSTAKES WORKS

NO PURCHASE NECESSARY

To enter each drawing, complete the appropriate Official Entry Form or a 3" by 5" index card by hand-printing your name, address and phone number and the trip destination that the entry is being submitted for (i.e., Caneel Bay, Canyon Ranch or London and the English Countryside) and mailing it to: Get Away From It All Sweepstakes, P.O. Box 1397, Buffalo, New York 14269-1397.

No responsibility is assumed for lost, late or misdirected mail. Entries must be sent separately with first class postage affixed, and be received by: 4/15/92 for the Caneel Bay Vacation Drawing, 5/15/92 for the Canyon Ranch Vacation Drawing and 6/15/92 for the London and the English Countryside Vacation Drawing. Sweepstakes is open to residents of the U.S. (except Puerto Rico) and Canada, 21 years of age or older as of 5/31/92.

For complete rules send a self-addressed, stamped (WA residents need not affix return postage) envelope to: Get Away From It All Sweepstakes, P.O. Box 4892, Blair, NE 68009.

© 1992 HARLEQUIN ENTERPRISES LTD.   SWP-RLS

- -

"GET AWAY FROM IT ALL" SWEEPSTAKES

HERE'S HOW THE SWEEPSTAKES WORKS

NO PURCHASE NECESSARY

To enter each drawing, complete the appropriate Official Entry Form or a 3" by 5" index card by hand-printing your name, address and phone number and the trip destination that the entry is being submitted for (i.e., Caneel Bay, Canyon Ranch or London and the English Countryside) and mailing it to: Get Away From It All Sweepstakes, P.O. Box 1397, Buffalo, New York 14269-1397.

No responsibility is assumed for lost, late or misdirected mail. Entries must be sent separately with first class postage affixed, and be received by: 4/15/92 for the Caneel Bay Vacation Drawing, 5/15/92 for the Canyon Ranch Vacation Drawing and 6/15/92 for the London and the English Countryside Vacation Drawing. Sweepstakes is open to residents of the U.S. (except Puerto Rico) and Canada, 21 years of age or older as of 5/31/92.

For complete rules send a self-addressed, stamped (WA residents need not affix return postage) envelope to: Get Away From It All Sweepstakes, P.O. Box 4892, Blair, NE 68009.

© 1992 HARLEQUIN ENTERPRISES LTD.   SWP-RLS

"GET AWAY FROM IT ALL"

Brand-new Subscribers-Only Sweepstakes

OFFICIAL ENTRY FORM

This entry must be received by: April 15, 1992
This month's winner will be notified by: April 30, 1992
Trip must be taken between: May 31, 1992—May 31, 1993

YES, I want to win the Caneel Bay Plantation vacation for two. I understand the prize includes round-trip airfare and the two additional prizes revealed in the BONUS PRIZES insert.

Name _____

Address _____

City _____

State/Prov. _____ Zip/Postal Code _____

Daytime phone number _____
                           (Area Code)

Return entries with invoice in envelope provided. Each book in this shipment has two entry coupons — and the more coupons you enter, the better your chances of winning!
© 1992 HARLEQUIN ENTERPRISES LTD.   1M-CPN